KINGPIN WIFEYS VOLUME 6

BY

K. ELLIOTT

CONTENTS

KINGPIN WIFEYS II,
Part 5: God Is For Us

Chapter 1

CRAIG JUMPED TO HIS FEET AND SAID, "WHAT THE HELL are you doing here?"

Jada ignored his silly ass. She wanted to slap the fuck out of him and said, "So, damn! It has come down to this. You're fucking trannies!" She chuckled then turned to Miss America who was clearly offended by Jada's use of the word tranny.

Jada said, "I'm about to go off in this motherfucker and it has nothing to do with you. So don't get offended." But it was too late. She was already offended but she could see that Jada was pissed. Miss America stood there huffing with her hands on her hips. Her mascara was running. It had been a very rough night.

Jada faced Craig again. Their eyes locked as she examined him. The once handsome white man was thin, unkempt and seemed almost fragile. An expensive shirt swallowed his frail body. He wore scuffed, blue and white Pumas. What a hot-ass mess, Jada thought.

Jada said, "I really can't stand yo ass."

Craig recognized the hurt in her eyes. "I need help. Everybody knows that." He threaded a hand through his hair.

"I don't give a damn about you needin' help."

Miss America clasped her hands behind her back and rocked from side to side impatiently. She could tell that these two shared a complicated history. They'd fucked and were possibly old lovers. "I'll be out in the hallway."

Jada said to her, "Don't worry. He's not going anywhere."

When the door closed, she turned to Craig. "Why'd you do it?"

"They were going to get him anyway. It was just a matter of time and you know it." Craig said.

Jada was about to sit on the edge of the bed before remembering this wasn't her room and she knew that Craig and that goddamned tranny had been doing God-knows-what on the bed. She hated to even think about it. There was a chair beside the desk in the corner. She marched right past Craig's ass and sat at the desk.

"They were going to get him. What don't you understand about that?" Craig said.

"I'll tell you what I do understand." She balled her fist. "I understand that a coke head, tranny-fucking doctor was looking for a way out and he wanted to save his own ass."

"What was I supposed to do? I couldn't go to prison. What about my kids?"

"You murdered that girl and you know it."

"And I never said I didn't."

"But you said that Shamari made you do it. You're the one that stuffed that girl's tits."

"I didn't mean for it to happen."

"But it did."

"You didn't think they weren't going to catch up with Shamari? For God's sake! He attempted to murder a federal witness!"

"He didn't do that."

"Well, he had somebody do it for him." Craig said.

Craig never thought he would see Jada again, and he knew how she felt about Shamari. He had often imagined how she must have felt. He'd read online that Shamari had received a life sentence and that he didn't need to worry about retaliation from him, but it didn't make him feel any better because he knew that when he lied on Shamari, he had hurt Jada in the process. Craig stood and paced as Jada's eyes followed him. She was not going to let him get out of the room.

Finally, he stopped pacing and said, "All you can think about is how you feel. What about how I felt?"

"How you felt? As a matter of fact, I really don't give a flying fuck how you felt. All I know is my man is in prison."

"Your man?" he said sarcastically.

"You know what I mean."

"I knew you cared about him, but you didn't love him. If you loved him, you wouldn't have fucked me. Jada, you're an expensive whore and that's why it shouldn't have surprised me that you ended up escorting."

Jada sprang from the chair, thinking did this motherfucker just say what she thought he said? Did he just call her a ho? She slapped the fuck out of him and he grabbed his jaw and attempted to restrain her. She slapped him again and said, "Don't put yo goddamned hands on me! First of all, I am not an escort. I came here for a friend because yo broke ass is trying to get out of paying."

"I'm going to pay. I'll have the rest of the money tomorrow."

Jada said, "If you ever fix your face to call me a ho again, I will kill you. I swear to God."

Craig laughed and said, "So, you're here so I won't leave?"

"Exactly!"

He laughed again and this pissed Jada the fuck off. God, she couldn't stand to look at this man. She couldn't stand his sarcastic-ass laugh. Why was this motherfucker so arrogant? He was a fuckin' cokehead. She swung wildly at him but missed and he grabbed her arms.

"Let me go, motherfucker." Jada said through clenched teeth.

TeTe barged into the room. "What's going on in here, Jada?"

"I'm going to kill this motherfucker if he don't let me go."

"You know him?"

"In a previous life."

TeTe's expression dulled. "Get your hands off of her or I swear to you I got goons waiting on me downstairs, and they'll come up here and toss your ass out the window and make it look like you jumped," TeTe said.

Craig released Jada and she slapped the fuck out him again. Jada's hand was now imprinted on Craig's jaw.

TeTe took Jada by the arm and whispered, "I need you to calm down before hotel security shows up. I could hear you as soon as I got off the elevator."

Jada was huffing. "I'm calm."

"Would you mind stepping into the hallway?"

"Rot in hell!" Jada screamed at Craig.

He laughed out loud again and he was just as sarcastic as ever.

When Jada was outside the room, TeTe revealed a pink 9mm. "So, you were saying that you were not going to pay all the money?"

"I never said that."

"Oh, it must have been a misunderstanding." TeTe smiled and stuffed the gun in the black crocodile Louis Vuitton bag.

"It was."

Chapter 2

IT WAS FORTY-THREE DEGREES AND THE AIR CONDITIONER was on full blast inside the interrogation room. Black had his arms tucked inside his T-shirt to provide some type of warmth but a short cop with a small afro named Stanton said, "I need you to take your arms out from underneath your shirt."

Black did exactly what the man asked and said, "It's your world, Boss Man. I just live in it."

Black sat at the short cafeteria-styled table surrounded by cops just like he'd done so many times before. Ever since he was a juvenile he'd been sitting there, and every time they interrogated him, he'd offer the same piece of information. Nothing. Nothing at all.

The three cops, Stanton, Kearns and Williams, stared at Black before breaking the silence.

Stanton asked, "So, where were you on May 18th at 6pm?"

"Hell, I don't know. I can't tell you where I was three days ago."

"Do you know Melvin Beatty?"

"Who?"

"Melvin Beatty, a.k.a. Popcorn."

"I'd have to see a picture of him."

Kearns presented a black and white mugshot of thirty-one-year-old Popcorn.

Black said, "I've seen him a few times."

"You've done business with him a few times, you mean."

"I don't know what you're talking about. I've seen you a few times," Black said, "but it don't mean I've done any kind of business with you. What kind of business are you referring to, sir?"

"Black, don't give me that bullshit. You know damn well what I'm talking about. You're a goddamned drug dealer. The only business you've ever known."

"Maybe Popcorn is a drug dealer but I'm a professional gambler."

"Have you ever gambled with Popcorn?" Williams asked.

Kearns turned to his partner and said, "Don't feed into his bullshit. He's a dope boy and that's all he's ever been."

"What if I told you that you were seen leaving Popcorn's house shortly after the murder?" Kearns said.

"Me?" Black sounded surprised.

"Yes you, motherfucker." Williams said.

"Who said I was?"

"Your baby mother."

"Was she there too?"

"You're a smart ass."

"Look man, are you accusing me of murder?"

"That's exactly what we're accusing you of. So if you want to, go ahead and admit it and maybe we can get you a deal." Williams said.

Black wanted to laugh at the silly motherfucker for even thinking that he would ever admit to anything. But more than that, he wanted to tell him to back up because his breath smelled like shit.

Kearns said, "I can tell you right now that he's not going to say a word. He's not going to talk. He's never said one word. He's been breaking the law since he was fourteen years old. He knows how to game the system."

"I told you I wasn't saying shit until my lawyer was here. I've already said too much."

Black was tapping the table. Not because he was afraid

or nervous but because he was bored. He'd called his attorney and Joey Turch had said he was about to go to Florida to see his parents. Black had told him to bring his ass downtown right away. When Joey Turch stepped inside the interrogation room, he asked the police to give him a minute with his client.

Turch was much thinner than Black remembered. He was wearing an expensive, grey, pinstriped Versace suit and had a spray tan. His hair was moussed and spiked. Black didn't like that look on him at all. He looked cheap and shady, but Black knew that if anybody could get him off, it was Joey Turch.

Turch sat across from Black and said, "Goddamn it, Tyrann. What the hell have you gotten into this time?"

Black made eye contact with his attorney. He wanted to cry and if Joey wasn't in the room and if the camera wasn't on him, he would have done exactly that.

"You want to tell me what happened?"

"Nothing happened."

"Something fuckin' happened or you wouldn't be charged with triple homicide. Did you do it?"

Black stared at the camera that was situated in the top right-hand corner of the room.

"The camera has been turned off." Joey Turch and Black made lingering eye contact and Turch said, "Did you do it?"

Nothing from Black.

"Look, you're going to have to talk to me and tell me the truth or I'm leaving right now because I can't help you."

"I didn't murder anyone, but I was with the man that did."

Turch looked confused.

"So you were at the scene of the crime?"

"Yeah, I was there. My friend was the triggerman. He pulled the trigger. He killed the three men."

"Why? What happened?"

"A deal that went wrong." Black dropped his head and though Turch was his attorney, he felt like was on The First 48. He felt like he was telling on a man that had been loyal to him, but he had to tell his attorney the truth.

"Yeah, I was inside the house making the deal."

"And you were about to get robbed?"

"No, not really. Well, I was selling some bad shit and the guy found out. Thought I was trying to beat him out of the bread and he wanted to kill me. He was going to kill me."

Turch ran his finger through his moussed hair. His fingers were now greasy and sticky.

"Damn it, Tyrann! Why were you selling bad shit?"

"I didn't know it was bad."

"What do you mean you didn't know it was bad?" Joey Turch had represented the worst of the worst and his clients loved him. They trusted him and he spoke their language when he needed to.

"Look, I got a new plug and it was the first time that I ever dealt with them."

"So the plug gave you some bad dope and you tried to sell it. But the people you were going to sell it to, found out it was no good and they were going to kill your ass but your friend squeezed first."

"L was in the car—."

"Who is L?"

"My friend that was with me."

"Continue."

"He got out to take a piss and he heard the commotion. He peeked inside the window and fired and killed the man who was pointing the gun at me."

"Where is L?"

"L is dead."

"Retaliation?"

"No something totally different."

"Tell me."

"He got murdered in a home invasion."

"So L was no church deacon, how do you know him?"

"Prison."

Joey Turch was deep in thought and Black was studying his face wondering what he was thinking. He knew Joey had always been cool with him and they had a mutual respect. Turch had to be thinking that he was a total fuck up.

" L is dead?"

"Yup."

"And you have a triple murder case that you have to fight. Damn, L might have gotten the best of this situation."

"Tell me about it."

"So after L murders the three people, what happens?"

"He throws me over his shoulder, takes me to the car and we drive away."

"Nobody saw you? No witnesses?"

"None."

"You're going to get indicted and I'm going to fight for you. That's all I can promise you."

"What about bond?"

"For triple murder? Nobody gets out on bond for triple murder."

"What happened to all this tough talk? I thought you were the best attorney in Atlanta?"

"Look, I'm sorry but nobody gets out on triple murder. You need to call Jesus for a bond, but I'm heading to Florida for my parent's wedding anniversary celebration. I'll speak with the D.A. when I return."

Chapter 3

THE PRISON YARD WAS CLOSED FOR HEAD COUNT. Correction officer Hankerson escorted Shamari to the hospital. When Shamari entered the small room in the hospital, he saw exactly who he had expected to see. Agents David Carroll and Scott Chandler were sitting at a table with two yellow legal pads and pens placed in the center of the table as if Shamari was going to snitch on Black. As soon as Shamari made eye contact with the cops, he turned to exit the room.

"Before you leave, you might want to hear us out."

"I ain't got shit to say."

"Just to let you know, your boy has been charged with triple homicide. It's over for him."

Shamari stopped in his tracks before turning and facing them again. Chandler was loading the yellow pads back into a briefcase. He hadn't expected Shamari to turn around.

"What are you talking about?"

"Tyrann has been charged with a triple homicide. He was picked up a few nights ago," Chandler said.

"Really? I don't believe you."

"Yes, it's true." Carroll said as Shamari approached the

table and sat opposite the two agents.

"If he's been charged with triple murder, what the fuck do you want with me?"

"Just want you to jump on the train. Tyrann is going down with or without you."

"Well, it will be without me."

"Look," Chandler said, the pen was out and he was flicking it again. He scribbled a line on the yellow paper to make sure it was working. "Brooks, we know you didn't deserve the time. We want to help you. We want to get you out of here."

"Ten years is still a long motherfucking time."

"Maybe you won't have to do ten years. Maybe you can get immediate release."

"And have the whole city questioning my street cred? Get the fuck out of here."

Chandler and Carroll stood at the same time. Chandler placed the pad and pen back into the briefcase. Chandler made eye contact with Shamari who was still seated and he said, "Brooks, you know how to reach us."

Shamari said, "What if I can give you something else? Some better information?"

Carroll said, "What?"

"Government corruption."

"What are you talking about?"

"I have information about a government official accepting bribes."

Both of the agents sat down at the same time.

"Who is the official?"

"The mayor."

"What do you know and how do you know it?" Chandler said.

"I'm friends with his daughter," Shamari lied. Black was friends with the daughter but they didn't need to know that.

"What else can you tell us? Who is his daughter?"

"I need an attorney."

"What are you talking about? Making sure your attorney is present? You contacted us. We didn't contact you the first time," Chandler said.

Carroll said, "Have your attorney call us and let's schedule a time to meet."

____

Chapter 4

INSIDE FRESH'S NEW TOWNHOME, HE WALKED BAREFOOT on his beautiful bamboo floors with his iPhone in his hand. He was peeking in on Jada's Instagram and he was furious. He was staring at a picture of two plates of food and it was hashtagged Houston's. It was obvious to him that this bitch was out with a man. Fresh scrolled through the rest of her pictures. Pictures of the Hawks game and the shooting range. It was that clown-ass dude that she was with at the basketball game. He logged out of Instagram, jumped into his car and headed over to her hotel. He made his way to her room and banged on the door. She opened and was wearing a pair of running shorts and a pink T-shirt with the words 'God is the Plug" in wintergreen letters.

With hands on her hips, she said, "What the fuck are you doing coming over here this time of morning?"

"Can I come in?"

She stepped aside and he barged right in. She shut the door and turned to face him. "So, now do you want to tell me what this is all about?"

"Who the fuck is he, Jada?"

"Who the fuck is who?"

"Who was the guy I saw you with the other night at the basketball game?"

She laughed and said, "So you were there and didn't speak?"

"Look, I didn't want to cause any problems." Fresh lied. The real reason he didn't speak was because he didn't want Jada to see Q out with a woman who wasn't Starr.

"Why would it cause any problems? You told me that we were just friends and that you didn't want anything but a friendship." She laughed and sat on the bed. "Oh, so you mad now?"

"Not mad. Just asking you a question."

"But you have no right to ask me shit. You ain't my man, and you made it quite clear that you wasn't trying to be my man."

He sat on the bed beside her, eyeing her breasts imprinted through the shirt. He was trying hard not to be turned on by her, but it was so hard. She was a sexy motherfucker. Now he was thinking about the guy at the game getting what was rightfully his.

"Is he your man?"

"You have no right to ask me shit." She laughed and said, "I thought you were a player, Fresh?"

"I never said one time that I was a player. You seem to think that I'm a player."

"Look, Fresh." She stood from the bed and made her way into the bathroom and gargled some mouthwash. "Let's get one thing clear. Just like I don't have a right to tell you who you can and can't fuck with, you have no right in telling me what the fuck I can and can't do. Understand?"

Fresh sat there on the edge of the bed looking like a defeated man. She was right. He was doing the same thing that he told her she had no right to do. He had to sort out his feelings. He didn't know if he was jealous. Was he pissed because she was with someone else and he didn't want her to have somebody else?

He raised his head and made eye contact with her and said, "You're right, Jada. I have no right to tell you what the fuck to do."

"I'm glad you realize that."

"I guess I'm jealous."

"If it makes you feel better. I'm not with this guy. I just met him."

"You like him?"

"I do."

"Look, Jada." He paused and she plopped right down on the bed again and he was staring at her boobs again. She knew he was looking, but she didn't mind. He lost his train of thought and she laughed.

"What was you about to say?" Jada asked.

"I was about to say that if he makes you happy, I think you should give the guy an opportunity."

That's not what Jada wanted to hear. She wanted Fresh but she didn't want to seem desperate or needy. "You think so?"

"I do."

"What do you want?"

"I don't know what I want."

She smiled and said, "Well, if you want me, you better come and get me."

"I do want you."

"Well, what are you afraid of?"

"I don't know."

"Take a chance. You might find love."

"And that's what I'm afraid of."

She saw him still staring at her breasts. She removed her T-shirt so he could get a better view of her nipples and she said, "You want me?"

"I do."

"Come here."

He grinned before placing her left tit in his mouth.

Chapter 5

A POD IS A GROUP OF PRISON CELLS WITH A COMMON
area where the inmates are sometimes allowed to converse,
play cards, watch TV and bullshit. Black was thrown into a
pod with eighty other inmates. The pod consisted of forty
rooms with two men to each cell. Black stepped into the pod
and sitting at a desk was a fat correctional officer named
Manley. Manley handed him some toothpaste, a toothbrush
and a bar of soap and a towel.

"Where is the deodorant?" Black asked.

"Budget cuts, bruh." Manley shrugged.

"So what am I supposed to do about funky armpits?"

"You can either borrow some, wait till you go to the store
on Thursday or go without. You have options." Manley
laughed.

"That's fucked up." Black mumbled, not wanting Manley
to hear him.

Manley said, "That's life."

Black had been assigned to room twenty-seven, and as he
was approaching his room, someone called out his name. He
turned and saw a dude named Cato from his neighborhood.
Cato was a short stocky guy. He had a pear-shaped head and

huge lips. He and Black had known each other since they were about six years old. And they both had the title of the baddest little kids in the neighborhood.

The older boys would make them fight each other—sometimes Cato would win, and sometimes Black would win. When they were about thirteen, they started hanging out with each other and even stole a car together. They had gotten arrested together for the stolen car. But Cato had moved out of the hood and Black would see him here and there over the years. Cato had started selling Molly and eventually did prison time.

Black was happy to see his friend. Cato was the kind of guy that was very animated when he talked. He'd spit and touched your chest and his favorite phrase was "You feel me?"

Cato approached Black and said, "If it isn't Tyrann Massey."

Black grinned and said, "Cato Wilson."

Black hadn't seen Cato in a very long time. The two men embraced and Cato asked, "What room are you in?"

"Twenty-seven."

"I'm in twenty-nine," Cato said. "I'll get you some soap, deodorant and toothpaste and bring it to your room, so you won't have to use that bullshit that Manley gave you."

Black was happy that Cato had offered to bring him some deodorant because there was no way he was going to make it until it was time to go to the store.

Black entered his room and introduced himself to his roommate—a white dude named Ronnie. Ronnie was a tall gangly biker, with long brown hair and tattoos on his knuckles. He looked like the kind of white boy that would fuck you up if he needed to.

Ronnie shook Black's hands and said, "I got two rules in this room."

"And they are?" Black asked staring at the big-ass white boy thinking about what he would have to do to fuck this white boy up if they got into it. He was taller and more muscular than Black. Black knew he would have to cheat. Perhaps grab his balls. Kick his shin. Bust the motherfucker across the head with a mop wringer. Or get him while he was asleep. He hoped it didn't come down to that but Ronnie struck him as the type of motherfucker who thought he owned the cell.

Ronnie said, "The first rule is you stay out of my goddamned business."

"The second?"

"I stay out of yours."

"Fine with me."

"Seriously. I don't like anybody talking about me or trying to meddle in my business."

"I can understand that." Black was making up his bed when Cato knocked on the door and stepped inside. He walked past Ronnie and handed Black the deodorant.

Ronnie said to Cato, "Is this your homeboy?"

Cato turned and faced him. "It is. Why?"

Ronnie laughed and said, "Calm down, little guy. I was just asking because you're in room twenty-nine with my friend John. Let's ask the cop if y'all can switch rooms."

"Good idea," Cato said.

Later that evening after count they exchanged rooms and Cato was in the room with Black on the bottom bunk.

Black sat on the bottom bunk thinking how in the hell was he going to get himself out of this situation and if he didn't get out of this shit, how long would he be gone. He thought back to the last conversation he had with his Dad about leaving the game alone. At that moment, he wished he'd stopped but by the time he'd spoken with his father, the cops were already looking for him.

Cato was lying on the top bunk checking out the XXL eye candy. He clutched his dick and was about to ejaculate, before reminding himself that Black was in the room with him. He set the magazine down but knew that he would get back to that later for sure.

"Black, what are you doing down there?" Cato said.

"Man, just thinking."

"About what?"

"How I fucked up."

"I know you said you fucked up, but how did you fuck up? What happened, bruh? Why are you in here?"

"Triple murder, but I ain't do it. One of my homies did it."

"Well, is it one of those situations where he did and you were with him and they want you to roll on him?"

"Naw. Nothing like that. I don't feel like talking about it right now."

"I'm in here on some bullshit, too."

He didn't have to say that. Everybody in jail was in there on some bullshit. Nobody is guilty. All the times Black had been in jail, he'd never met anyone that said, 'Hey, I did what they said I did.'

"I was living with a friend and the Twelve came to his house." Twelve was code for police, mostly used in trap houses.

Cato hopped down off the bed. "You feel me?" Cato then peeked out into the common area trying to make sure nobody was listening. "I wasn't even at the house. You feel me? But they found drugs in the room where my stuff was and they're trying to pin it on me."

"What did the owner of the house say?"

"He ain't saying shit. They charged him with guns and shit. They ain't charge me with guns, but I gotta get out this motherfucker befo' they hit me with a gun charge. You feel me?"

"What is your bond?"

"My bond's a hundred thousand dollars and I need ten to get out and I would have had it. Matter of fact, they took fifty-five hundred from my room. I was rolling, my nigga, but they took everything I had."

Black sat up, thinking fifty-five hundred dollars hardly qualified as high-roller status. "So, your folks ain't got no property or nothing that they can put up to get you out."

"Black, you know me. They ain't got shit. You feel me? You been knowing me all my life and we ain't never had shit. You feel me?"

"Damn."

Cato sat beside Black on the bed. "Look, Black, I know we ain't really fuck with each other on the street, but we've never been enemies. Except when we were kids fighting every day. But you know me, and you know I'm a stand-up dude. You feel me?" He patted Black on the chest. Black didn't like anybody touching him and the motherfucker saying, 'You feel me?' was getting on Black's goddamned nerves.

"So what are you getting at?"

"Look, I know you was making money and lots of it. You know the streets talk and all over Atlanta people been talking about how much bread you got. You feel me?"

"What's the point? Okay, I got a little bit of money."

Cato looked Black straight in the eye and said, "Look, man. I need you to help me get up out this motherfucker. If you can."

Black didn't respond. Was this man serious? Cato wanted Black to give him ten thousand dollars to get out?

"If you can't do it, I'm cool. We still good. You feel me? But I'm just saying, if you can get me out, I would appreciate it, big bruh. You know I got kids and shit. You feel me? And they need me home."

Black sighed and said, "I tell you what. If I get out of here, I'll get you out. I promise."

"What if you don't get out, big bruh? You got some serious charges. You feel me? I'm just gonna keep it one hundred with you. With those kind of charges you got…"

Black said, "I feel ya."

"So, what you're saying is if you don't get out. I don't get out?"

"I mean, if they absolutely tell me that I'm not getting out, I'll still get you out. But let me have my day in court first before I think about helping you."

Cato said, "I feel ya."

Black stood and was about to go into the common area to use the payphone when Cato said, "How long you going to be out there?"

"About ten minutes. Just gotta use the phone. Why?"

"Can you stay out there for twenty minutes?" He held up the XXL eye candy and said, "I got work to do. You feel me?"

They both laughed their asses off.

Chapter 6

THE LAST SEVEN MONTHS FOR CRAIG MATTHEWS HAD been like living in hell. He'd lost everything that he'd ever cared about. He was rarely in touch with his wife and kids nowadays. He lost his mistresses. He'd even lost his license to practice cosmetic surgery and he was staying in a rundown home that sat right across the street from a trailer park. He ended up giving underground butt implants to strippers, trannies and gays to support his coke habit. He'd never thought that he would ever sleep with a tranny and he hadn't intended to, but it happened. And after that, he had starting thinking there was little difference between a transsexual woman and a real woman—well, except that man-part.

His first time was with a tranny named Persia. She was six feet tall with skin the color of caramel latte and hair that reached the top of her ass. Their first encounter happened after he'd snorted an eight ball of cocaine and he was horny but he didn't have enough money to buy a woman. Persia had begged him for another round of ass injections, but she didn't have the money. He was more expensive than the other black market injectors, but he was better than all them because unlike them, he injected real fat into the asses of his patients and molded them into a shelf.

He knew exactly what they desired. He had been around enough black women to know what they thought was a nice ass. He called Persia and made her a proposition. He wanted sex, but he wasn't going to sleep with a man. The way he saw it was that if he only got oral sex, it would be okay. He rationalized that he wasn't gay because after all she looked like a woman. Then he got attached and he began to spend more and more time with Persia. It got to the point where a regular woman couldn't turn him on any more. He'd tried several times to sleep with biological women but he could no longer climax. Persia was killed in a car accident and he had resorted to hooking up with escorts.

He was tired of living like some goddamned peasant while his wife was living in the lap of luxury.

Craig had phoned Miss America and said he wanted to see her. He asked her to bring a friend but she was adamant about not seeing his cheap ass until he sent her a grand upfront through PayPal. They both had to be careful that TeTe didn't find out. Miss America knew that if TeTe find out she was meeting clients behind TeTe's back, it wouldn't be good. Rumor was that a girl named Naomi had been seeing a client behind TeTe's back and TeTe showed up at her home and ordered her kids to lock themselves in their bedroom while her henchmen held Naomi down and TeTe beat her with a whip.

Miss America and Fy-Head sat right across from Craig on a dingy brown sofa. He offered them water, soda or beer and Fy-Head asked for a Bud Light.

After he passed her the beer, he sat across from them and said, "I wanted to know if you would be interested in helping me do something."

"What?"

He stood and made his way over to the window. He peeked outside and then closed the blinds tightly. He popped the top off the can of soda as he sat back down across from the two trannies.

"I know you're thinking that I brought you over for some freaky sexy party."

"No. We really didn't have sex the last time I saw you because you didn't want to pay."

"You don't have to keep reminding me of what happened." The first time they met up, Craig had snorted so much coke that his penis had shriveled up and he couldn't even receive head.

Fy-Head sipped more beer and said, "I'm wondering why the hell am I here. I don't have time for this bullshit. I'm going to tell you right now, I have HIV, so if you want to, you'll have to take your chances."

Craig laughed and said, "This meeting has nothing to do with that."

"So what do you want?"

He stood and paced then ran over to the window and checked the blinds again.

Fy-head took another sip of the beer and said, "Will you tell me what the fuck is going on? You're making me nervous, motherfucker."

'I know," Craig said then moseyed over to the sofa again. When he was seated, he looked both trannies in the eyes and said, "Do you know any killers?"

"What!" Fy-Head said.

"Listen, I need somebody offed. I mean, I need them murdered but I need a professional to do it."

Miss America said, "Look, I love my freedom too much for shit like this."

"I'm not asking you if you yourself are a killer. I am wondering if you know anybody that is down on their luck and could use fifteen thousand dollars."

Fy-Head said, "Did you say fifteen thousand dollars?"

"Why would anybody believe you?" Miss America said. "As a matter of fact, I don't believe yo cheap ass got fifteen thousand dollars to your name." She looked around and said, "You live in this cheap-ass house. You have that piece of shit Honda Accord in the driveway. You ain't got no money."

"You can ask Jada. I was very well off."

Fy-Head said, "Who the fuck is Jada?"

"That bird TeTe had with her the first time we met her."

"Hmmph. I don't ever wanna see that bitch again." Fy-head rolled her eyes.

Miss America said, "Don't believe shit this motherfucker has to say. He is a wannabe. This clown don't got no real paper."

Fy-Head was eyeing the Breitling on Craig's wrist and said, "Well, he has something. How much that watch cost?"

"Twelve thousand dollars," Craig said.

"So, you had some bad luck? What kind of bad luck because judging by the watch you've had money before?"

"I used to be the best cosmetic surgeon in Atlanta before they took my license away."

Fy-head said, "Wait a minute. I knew you looked familiar. You was the guy that stuffed that girl's breast implants with coke and she died, right?"

"Heroin."

"Yeah, I knew you looked familiar."

"The death was accidental."

"And they took your license?"

"Yeah and my wife divorced me and took everything that I had and here I am."

Miss America said, "Well, I don't understand. If you don't have any money, how in the hell are you going to pay someone fifteen grand?"

"I got two butt implant jobs and soon as I'm done, I can give you the money if you are serious about doing the job," Craig said as he looked at Fy-Head.

Fy-Head rolled her neck and said, "Wait a minute, motherfucker. I ain't never said that I was going to kill anybody. You can get that out yo mind right now."

"I thought we had an agreement?"

"Motherfucker, did I say we had an agreement?"

"So you can't use the fifteen grand?"

"A bitch can definitely use the money." Fy-head sipped her drink and said, "So who are you trying to kill? Who do you want murdered, good doctor, and why?"

Craig said, "It's a long story but if you have time..."

"We have time."

Chapter 7

BLACK HAD BEEN REMOVED FROM HIS POD AFTER BEING told that they had a witness that could possibly identify him in a line-up. They brought him in along with four other inmates and the witness told the investigators that Black was positively at the murder scene. Now, the investigators would try to match is DNA.

Black was lying on his bunk trying to get some rest when the correctional officer came over. "You've got an attorney visit, Black."

When Black stepped into the attorney's visitation room, Joey Turch was waiting on him. He said, "I got some good news and some bad news. Which do you want first?"

"When are you going to get me the fuck out of here? That's all I want to know. I want to get the fuck out. If you can't get me the fuck out, I don't care what news you have first."

"Stay positive."

"Look, you take your ass back there and let them feed you that bullshit and let's see you keep a positive attitude."

"Do you want the good or bad news first?"

"What's the bad news?" The air-conditioned room was cold as fuck and he was wearing slippers with his orange jumpsuit. They kept it cold in all parts of the jail and he was freezing his ass off day after day.

"The bad news is a witness identified you at the scene."

"What witness?"

"Porsha Thomas."

"I don't know who the fuck that is."

"Seventeen year-old girl. The seventeen-year-old man's girlfriend."

Black thought back to the day he and L were in the car and Popcorn's nephew and a fine-ass seventeen-year-old girl was walking down the sidewalk switching her young ass.

"Okay, if that is the bad news, what the fuck is the good news?"

"The good news is that she said you weren't the one that fired the gun. She said she witnessed a huge man with a bald head fire a shot through the window."

"Yeah that was L., the friend I was telling you about."

"She said she saw him carrying you out the door, he laid you down and shot the kid."

"Yes, it's true."

Joey Turch was lost in thought and suddenly he had an idea.

•   •   •

Black was in the interrogation room surrounded by Kearns and Williams before he broke down crying and said, "This is how it went. I was there to pick up two kilos of cocaine from this guy named Memphis."

Williams said, "Memphis?"

"Yeah, I ain't know his real name but I was there to pick up some coke from Memphis. Except I didn't bring the money because I didn't know him, plus I didn't have the money anyway." Black lied. But who would know when everybody was dead except him.

"Please continue," Williams said.

Black cracked his knuckles and said, "Can I have a cup of coffee?"

"Ain't no goddamned coffee." Williams was irritated.

"Damn, man! Why you get so bent out of shape?"

"This ain't no fuckin' TV show. You need to finish saying what you have to say."

Joey Turch said, "You will not talk to my client like this."

"You are the one that said your client wanted to speak to us. As far as I was concerned, there was nothing else to talk about. He will have his day in court."

"And there was no way in hell you were getting a conviction. There is no murder weapon and only one witness that said she didn't see him fire a shot."

Kearns said, "Continue please."

"When I realized that Memphis's coke wasn't real and he realized that I didn't have the money, he drew his gun and I screamed loud enough for my friend to hear. He peeked in and fired a shot that hit him in the back and killed him on contact."

Williams laughed and said, "So, you mean to tell me that you screamed loud enough for him to hear you when you were in the back of the house?"

"He was taking a piss. I swear to God, man. He heard me. I ain't got to lie." Black said, knowing damn well he needed to lie and this was exactly what he was doing. He had to lie to get out of this situation.

A fake teardrop cascaded down his jaw into his mouth. "I feel so fucked up telling on my partna."

"What's your friend's name, Tyrann, and where does he live?"

Black covered his face with his hands and said, "His name is Larry Harris. He is the guy that killed the three people. He is the one that you want, not me. He is the guy that the witness saw."

Williams said, "I've heard that name before. He was murdered."

Black was bawling in his seat again. This time, real tears were forming for his dead friend.

"We can't prosecute a dead man, Tyrann. This is bullshit, and you know it."

Black looked at Joey Turch and Turch grinned. Turch was toying with some expensive diamond cufflinks that cost the same as a month's salary for the detectives. They hated the prick and he had won against them more times than they could think of.

"Listen, you don't have enough evidence to make a murder case stick and you know it. Do you really want to go to trial and waste money on a case that you know you can't win?" Turch asked.

"We'll charge him with the coke that he was going to buy. Attempted possession."

Black made eye contact with his attorney who then said, "I want a word with my client."

The detectives left the room and Black said, "So, they're going to charge me with the coke?"

"Who cares? They know they can't make a case for the three bodies and they know the coke wasn't really coke. Don't worry about it."

"When am I going to get out of here?"

"I would say in a day or two. They are going to have to charge you with something or let you go."

Black looked up in the sky and said, "Thank God for this."

Chapter 8

JADA AND STARR SAT IN A BOOTH AT THE HOUSE OF Hookah on 14th Street sipping Mojitos and toking on hookah pipes when Jada said, "Hey, I want to tell you something but promise you won't tell anybody."

Starr took a toke from the hookah and said, "I promise."

Jada said, "Look, the other day I was looking in Fresh's phone and I saw where he'd sent Q a picture of a girl."

Starr sipped her drink. She didn't know how to respond. She knew that she didn't have a reason to get mad. She was the one that asked for the break.

Jada said, "I think Q is seeing the girl."

"How does the chick look?"

"I ain't going to lie, she beautiful. Not as beautiful as you though."

Starr laughed and said, "I can't believe I asked you that."

"Starr, you're human with human emotions. Wanting to know how she looks is not a stupid question."

"It sounds so high school."

Jada took a pull off the pipe.

Starr said, "How do you know he's seeing her?"

"The chick that you saw Fresh with texted him and said

that Chanel said thanks for introducing her to Q."

"Her name is Chanel?"

"Yeah."

"I always liked that name."

"She has nothing on you. I'm telling you. She looks a little stuck up."

Starr was dying inside. But she had to keep a straight face. She was trying to gather her words but all she could think about was this Chanel girl and the fact that Jada had just said that Chanel was a cute girl. But Starr knew that Q had good taste in women. Hell, he wanted her.

Jada flagged the waitress and ordered more drinks and she noticed that Starr was staring off into space. Jada moseyed her way to Starr's side of the table and embraced her.

Jada held her for a while. "It's going to be okay. You don't have to talk about it if you don't want to."

"But I want to." Starr took another drag off the pipe. "I just want to know if he'd met her when Fresh met Brianna."

"He'd just met her. It was very recent according to the date on the text."

"So he met her after I suggested that we take a break. I'm mad as fuck but there ain't shit I can say." She poured more liquor.

•   •   •

Black was charged with attempted purchase of cocaine and he was bonded out. His attorney had warned him that it was far from over and there was still a very good possibility that he would be charged with murder later. But for now he was a free man.

His first order of business was to get a new burner since the police had his old cell phone. His sister Rashida picked him up from jail. When she learned that the murder charges had been dropped against him, she agreed to rent him a car. A Chevy Lumina.

Since he didn't have TeTe's number, he drove over to her house and she was happy when she opened the door. She greeted him with a warm hug and but he could tell something was bothering her.

"You have bad news, don't you?" Black said.

"What makes you say that?"

"The expression on your face."

"There is a problem."

"What the fuck is it? Tell me?"

"You don't know, do you?"

"I don't know shit. This is the first place that I came when I got out of jail."

"I went to your house and went down to the basement just like you asked me and there was nobody in the cage. The cage was empty."

"Impossible."

TeTe said, "Look, baby, I did what you asked me to do. I drove to your house, I went to the basement and there was nobody in the cage. Nobody."

Black paced and he knew by her tone that she was being truthful. She had no reason to lie. He sat on an armchair and rested his arms between his legs and said, "How did this happen?"

She sat down and said, "Can you explain to me, what in the fuck was going on and why in the hell was this man captured in the first place? That was some old weird sex slave shit. I mean I saw panties and baby oil. All kinds of shit was going on."

He looked up at her and said, "The man in the basement was the man that had killed Lani and I wanted to make the rest of his life a living hell."

"By fucking him and keeping him as a sex slave?"

"Not my sex slave."

"Somebody was fucking in that basement."

"It was my friend L."

"Who the fuck is L?"

"My friend was the one that was fucking the tranny that we met in the Waffle House."

TeTe was satisfied with that answer.

Black said, "How did he escape?"

"Look, I didn't even know you had a motherfucker in your basement, so you know I ain't have shit to do with it."

"I know, babe. I'm just thinking out loud. I gotta get some stuff from that house and then get out fast. Whoever broke him out of the house will be back."

"I have a place in Sandy Springs that I was trying to rent to Jada."

"Is it nice?"

"Yeah."

"I'll take it."

She laughed and said, "You don't even know how it looks."

"I don't give a fuck how it looks. I need somewhere to go."

"If you want the place, it's yours."

Their eyes met and held for a while. Neither of them said a word. Black removed his pants and his big black dick was pointing at her. She plopped down on her knees. He placed his manhood on her lips and she took him deep inside her mouth.

"He missed you."

She removed her clothes and finger fucked herself while she gave him head. Black was smiling at the sight of her beautiful ass giving him head.

•   •   •

Nana called Black and said that he had been receiving calls. He took the names of the four callers. One was from L's baby mama, one was from Cato in the county jail and one was from Shamari. Shamari had left a number for Black to call him. He also remembered that he had promised Cato he would pay for Cato's bond as soon as he moved into his new place.

The fourth caller was from somebody named Amber. Nana said that she'd called three times. Black didn't know anyone named Amber but he called the number and someone picked up on the fifth ring.

"Who da hell keeps calling my phone from a private number?" Fetty Wap's Swing My Way played in the background.

"Is this Amber?"

"And who the hell is dis calling me by my government name?"

"This is Black."

"Oh my bad, Black." Then she said to someone in the room. "Can you turn the music down?

The volume of the music lowered and Black said, "Amber, where I know you from?"

"This is Champagne from Club Nikki's."

"Oh damn! Why didn't you say Champagne?"

"I dunno. Something just didn't seem right telling your Nana that my name was Champagne."

Black was laughing his ass off. "I feel ya. What's up?"

"Just calling you to put you up on something. Can I see you? Hell, might wanna get me some. You still packing?"

Somebody turned the volume of the radio back up. More Trap music.

She yelled out, "Can't you see I'm on the goddamned phone? Kids, I tell ya."

"I ain't know you had kids. "

"You know, I got a sixteen year old and a twelve year old. Started having them early."

"Me and you both. Damn, where were they when we were kicking it?"

"Oh, they were still in Saint Louis with my mama. You remember when I was fuckin' with you? I had just moved here."

"That's right."

"So just let me know when you have time."

"You can't tell me over the phone?"

"I can but I would rather tell you in person."

"Let's meet at Houston's across from Lennox." There was no way in the fuck Black was going to meet this woman, at her home, especially, since he hadn't seen her in years. But why would she call Nana. One thing that Black knew was that strippers knew gangsters and they knew exactly what was going on in the streets.

•   •   •

Black spotted Fresh and a Mexican man, sitting in a booth as soon as he entered the restaurant. He moseyed his way past the booth and made eye contact with Fresh. They acknowledged each other with a greeting.

Black looked at the Mexican man and said, "Pardon my interruption." Then Black gave Fresh his phone number and then made his way to the back of the restaurant to wait on Champagne.

Champagne was wearing a black skirt and her hair was in a blue bob. The lower level of her mouth had tattoos of two angels. Black remembered her telling him that those tattoos were for her brother Koran and her father Kory. They had both been murdered execution style. She had left Saint Louis because six male members of her family had all been murdered in the last four years and she needed to come to Atlanta for a better life. She had always been cool with Black and Black thought she was a great person but she was just a bit too ghetto for Black. They sat in the back of the restaurant.

"You hungry?"

"I want a drink."

When the waitress appeared, Black ordered a shot of Hennessy and Champagne ordered a double.

After the server dropped the drinks off, Champagne said, "Black, you can't tell nobody what I'm about to tell you. If anybody learns that I told you this, I can get killed and I got my boys and nobody to raise them. Mama just had a stroke and she can't do it."

"Your secret is safe with me."

She downed that double shot and ordered another one and Black was getting impatient. He wanted to know what the fuck she had to say.

"Niggas is out to get you."

"What else is new?"

"So you knew already?"

"That's the story of my life, but what did you hear?"

"There are people wanting to know where you lay your head at, bruh."

"From you?"

"No not from me. From Sapphire."

"Sapphire? Who is that?"

"You know Sapphire. She worked with me at Folleys when I used to work there. Well, Sapphire said something about you had something to do with a dude named Shakur getting murdered. She wouldn't tell me all the details, but she said that one of the niggas vowed to kill you."

"Why did she tell you?"

"I don't know. We were together one night after the club and we were both rolling off Molly and to make a long story short, we fucked. But just to let you know, I don't get down like that. I don't fuck women unless I'm high."

Black was thinking he could care less if she fucked women or not. He just wished that she would get to the goddamned point and she could sense that he was getting annoyed.

She took a sip of her liquor while studying Black's irritated face and said, "So the morning after we fucked, she asked me if I knew you. I don't know why she asked me if I knew you when she know she's seen me and you talking in the club."

"Get to the point."

"I don't know. I just thought it was strange that she asked me that."

"She asked you if you knew me?"

"Yeah."

"Why did she ask you that?"

"I was about to tell you."

"Will you fucking tell me?" Black had got loud and the people at the next table were looking in their direction. "Look, I'm sorry for yelling."

Champagne leaned forward and said, "I'm trying to tell you that motherfuckers are trying to kill you."

"You told me that already, but who are they? What are their names?"

"I don't know their names."

"That's not going to do me any good."

"There was this one dude name Jabril. He wants you bad. He swears that you killed his brother."

"So you do know names?"

"I only know his name cuz Sapphire told me about him. Sapphire told me and said something about this chick named TeTe. They are going to get her. I asked but that's about all she told me. So I was just letting you know to be careful."

"Look, I appreciate you and if you hear anything else, let me know."

She was smiling with sparkling white teeth. She said, "So how you gonna pay me back?"

Black stared at her like she was crazy. "What do you think it's worth?"

"Some dick at least."

Black peeled off a thousand dollars and said, "I'm going to call you later."

•   •   •

Diego chugged down a glass of Scotch and said to Fresh. "Look I did some bad shit. Some very bad shit. I'm know some people would say that I'm not a good person. But you know my friend, I've made you and Q rich men."

Fresh said, "I know, but why did you murder Rico? He was like a big brother to me."

Diego sighed and then ordered another shot of scotch—a double. "Look, we cannot fix the past. I fucked up."

"You did. And you sent us bad product. What was that about? Why did you do that?"

"I wanted to cripple Q financially."

"But you didn't."

"I know and I know my cousin Gordo has given him product."

"How did you know that?"

"I know everything."

Fresh chomped down on a plate of fries, and though he told Q that he was going to work with Diego, he felt bad. But he knew that this was for the greater good.

"Let's not worry about what Q and Gordo got going on."

"Do I look worried?" He smiled, flashing those horsey veneers.

"You like Atlanta?"

"I love Atlanta. There is so much money to be made here." He reached over and grabbed one of Fresh's fries. Then his face got serious. "Can I tell you something?"

"Anything."

"Watch your back around Q."

"Q is my big brother."

"Q came to me a few months back and asked me if I could get someone to kill one of his good friends."

"What good friend?" Fresh stared at him and wondered what the hell Diego was talking about and if what Diego was saying was true, why didn't Q share the information with him?

"Someone named Trey. Did you know him?"

"Vaguely. He's from Atlanta, well he was from Atlanta. He's dead now."

"How?"

"His baby mama killed him."

Fresh ate some more fries and tried to digest what Diego was telling him. "Why would Q want Trey dead? They were like brothers."

"I don't know but I never met Trey, so you know I didn't just pull that name out of the sky."

"So why are you telling me this?"

"Just to let you know Q ain't no better than me. Just giving you a warning."

Fresh ate another fry and said. "So is that why you wanted to meet?"

"I wanted to meet because I got a thousand ki's for you if you still want to do business."

"Damn right."

• • •

Black was staked out across from Houston's, waiting on Fresh and the Mexican to leave the restaurant. The man that Fresh was with had to be the connect. Why would he be meeting with a Mexican? Not just any Mexican. Black could tell that he was a rich Mexican. Black had wanted to get in touch with Fresh as soon as he got out of jail. He wanted to tell him that the charges had been dropped to see if they could get back to work, but now that the connect was here, there was no need for all of that. Fresh came out as the restaurant valet pulled up with a cream-colored Bentley. Black witnessed Fresh hop into the car, and seconds later, the connect hopped into a white Aston Martin. Black trailed him to a convenience store. He knew that this could be his big break if he met the connect. There would be no need to use Fresh or Q. He would be on the same level as them. The connect jumped out of his car and Black approached him.

"Hey, you don't know me, but I'm Black."

"And I'm Mexican. What the fuck does that mean?"

"No, Black is my name."

"Okay…"

"Look, I was the guy that spoke to Fresh inside the restaurant."

"I don't get it. What do you want with me?"

"I think we can help each other."

"I'm listening."

"You got what I want and I got what you want."

"Look, I'm going to need you to get the fuck away from me right now. I'm someone that you don't want to fuck around with. Believe me."

"Okay, partner."

Chapter 9

AGENTS CARROLL AND CHANDLER USED THE INFORMATION Shamari had given them and determined that Sasha Anderson was the mayor's daughter. They contacted the FBI who already had an ongoing investigation into the mayor's dealings. Chandler and Carroll were able to track Sasha down, and surprisingly, she was very forthcoming about some of her dealings over the phone. She was also more than willing to help bring the mayor down.

Sasha sat across from Chandler and Carroll inside the Homeland Security office. Two agents from the FBI, Barry Daniels and James Sanders, joined in on the interview. Daniels was a tall black man with a baldhead and a diamond earring while Sanders was a white man with a graying beard.

When Sasha sat across from the four men, she asked, "Should I get an attorney?."

Sanders said, "That is your right, ma'am, but let me tell you before you go out and spend your money on an attorney, you've already admitted to knowing about the bribes and you've admitted to knowing a man that is connected to terrorists."

Sanders put his hands on her back and said, "We're going

to protect you."

"I know." She buried her head in her hands.

"Look, you don't need an attorney," Chandler said. "You have immunity papers saying that you will not be charged with a crime. We will not seize any of your personal assets. You're not going to prison and that's the main thing. There is nothing an attorney can help you with."

Sasha knew from watching The First 48 that they did not like it when you requested to see your attorney.

Sanders said, "What are you afraid of?"

"Nothing."

He finally said, "So, what changed? You said that you were willing to help."

"Nothing changed," she said.

Daniels made eye contact with her and there was a moment of sexual energy passing between the two of them. He was attracted to her and he knew she was attracted to him. If Sanders and the two Homeland Security agents weren't in the office, there was no doubt in his mind that they'd be fucking. He was getting that vibe from her.

"We need you to wear a recording device, get him to talk about the bribes that he's been taking and you're going to get immunity. That was the deal."

*   *   *

Q was surprised when security called and said that Starr was there to see him. He instructed the security guard to send her up. When she entered his place, she looked amazing. She was wearing a form fitting, blue pencil skirt and heels. Her hair was up and she looked much younger but she was still dressed sophisticated and stylish. He hadn't realized how much he had missed this woman. But he was smiling at her hard as hell as he embraced her.

He said. "I missed you."

"Did you now?"

"I did."

"I missed you too. I hate to admit it, but I missed you so much."

"So what brings you here?"

"Catch you at a bad time?"

"No. I was doing absolutely nothing. Nothing at all."

She smiled and she caught him staring at her tiny waist. She knew he wanted her at that moment and she felt wonderful that he was lusting after her.

"Would you like a drink?"

"Coffee."

"I've never seen you drink coffee."

"Tired, you know?" They made awkward eye contact before she sighed and turned away. "My body needs caffeine."

"No coffee, but I have some Coke."

"I'll take one. "

He disappeared into the kitchen and returned with a bottle of Coke and a cup of ice. He unscrewed the bottle for her and passed her the cup of ice. They both sat down. She sat on the sofa and he on the armchair across from her. He was staring at her like she was cake and ice cream—delicious and savory. He wanted to fuck her, but even more than that, he wanted to make love to her. He loved her and he missed her and he kept wondering if she was back to stay.

She poured the soda into the cup of ice and when the fizz settled, she sipped it. "So, what's new?" she asked.

"Nothing."

"No new girlfriend?"

"Nope."

"You dating anyone?"

"Wait a minute. I thought you wanted to take a break?"

"I do."

"So, if you want to take a break, what makes you think that you have the right to ask me anything?"

"Hey, I was just asking you a question. You don't have to answer it. I just know what that means."

"What does it mean?"

"What would it mean to you if you asked me if I was dating someone, and I refused to answer?"

"Yes, I've been on a date."

"You move fast."

"Look, that was nothing serious."

"Do you like her?"

"I like you."

She smiled and then sat her cup down. "I don't want you to see her anymore."

"If you tell me that we are off the break, I won't see her. If you don't, I'm going to see whoever I want to see."

"One more question."

"I didn't sleep with her."

"That's not what I was going to ask, but that's good to know."

"What do you want to know?"

"Was that the woman that called and hung up that night?"

"It wasn't her."

"How can you be so sure?"

"Because I didn't meet her until after you decided to take a break."

"What's her name?"

"Who?"

"Your little girlfriend."

"Starr."

"You know what I mean." She gulped down more soda.

He stood and began to pace. "I'm not going to tell you her name. It's not important." His eyes lit up. "But, if you tell me right now that we are not on break, I will delete her number from my phone and never call her again."

Starr stood and approached him. She draped her arms around his waist and rubbed his flat stomach. She laid her head on his chest.

He kissed her forehead then stroked her hair. "I missed the hell out of you."

"I missed you, too."

She released him, took a seat again and gulped down the remaining Coke straight from the bottle. Then she met his eyes and said, "I know you think I'm crazy."

He laughed but didn't respond. The truth was he did think she had a ton of issues but if he said that she was crazy, he knew that it would not be taken as a good thing. So he figured the best thing for him to do was to keep his thoughts to himself.

"You can say it."

"Would you like another Coke?" He tried to change the subject.

"No." She crossed her leg, exposing the bottom of her shoe. Six-inch Louboutins. She was so feminine and so classy. Chanel was beautiful too, but Chanel didn't possess that hood element that he so loved.

"I don't think you're crazy."

"Good." She smiled knowing damn well he was lying to her. Why wouldn't he think she was crazy? She had been acting like a crazy, insecure bitch. If she were him, she would think that she was bananas.

"Starr, I love you. I wish it wasn't the case, but I love you. You can't help who you fall in love with." He took a seat.

She stood up and made her way over to him. She took a seat on his lap and said, "I just don't want to be hurt."

His dick came alive and she stroked it through his jeans. Finally, unzipping them, she began rubbing the head.

Q grabbed her hand and said, "What are we doing?"

"I don't know."

"I don't know, either. I mean, one minute we're on break, and next minute you're over here stroking my dick. This is crazy to me."

"So, I am crazy?"

"No, I said this is crazy."

"I'm sorry," she said.

"It's okay."

"No, it's not." She stood and said, "Truth is that my trust issues with Trey have spilled over into this relationship and I don't trust you enough to allow you to love me, and I don't want you to be with nobody else. I'm sorry."

Q pulled her close and kissed her passionately before she pushed him away.

He said, "Just remember. I'm here if you need me."

She walked past him and he watched her ass sway as she approached the door. He wanted to fuck her right now and he cursed himself for not allowing himself to touch her.

Chapter 10

AT IHOP, A REDHEAD NAMED PAM TOOK BLACK AND Sasha's order. She ordered pancakes and turkey sausage and he had grits, scrambled eggs and toast. Sasha had called him and made it clear not to come to her place again. After the waitress dropped their food at the table, she said, "Where the fuck you been for the last couple of days?"

"I was in jail."

"In jail? In jail for what?"

Black spread some grape jelly on his toast and said, "It's a long story, man."

"Okay, you'll have to tell me about it some other time. I got news of my own."

Black was hoping like hell that this bitch wasn't about to say that she was pregnant. There was no way in the hell that he would allow her to keep the baby if this was the case. He didn't need any more children. That's for damn sure.

"What is the news?"

"I went to meet with the Feds"

Black's heart was beating like hell. He picked up his glass of orange juice and he could barely hold it. He was trembling so goddamned bad that when she noticed it, she laughed.

"Don't worry, babe. Nobody asked about you."

"Who was it? FBI? DEA? Homeland Security? Who the fuck was it?"

"It was the FBI, and they wanted to know about daddy. Wanted me to let them bug my condo and get him to discuss his dealings. The cash he's accepted for favors. I'm seriously thinking about doing it. He's taken so much away from me."

"I'm not big on snitching," Black said, "but that motherfucker needs to go down. I want him to leave you the fuck alone."

"I know. I just don't want this to come out. You know it's going to be all over the papers and the news."

"You ready for that?"

"I have to do it."

"Why do you feel like you have to do it?" Black said, not because he didn't want her to do it, he did. This man had tortured her, her whole goddamned life. If there was anyone that deserved to be in prison, it was him. Black was just curious about what she was thinking.

Tears formed in her eyes. She didn't feel like thinking about what her father had done. How he had robbed her of her life and her happiness. "Look, Black, I have to do it."

"I have an idea."

"I'm listening."

"I want you to tell them that you'll do it if they give Shamari Brooks a time cut. You know, let him out of prison."

"I'll call and ask them."

"You would do that for me?" Black smiled.

"Anything for you Daddy?"

He pulled her into his chest. He could feel her heartbeat and he said, "You're nervous."

"Yes."

"Why?"

"I don't know."

He handed her a gun. A snub nose .38.

"What is this for?"

"Just because."

"Because what?"

"Just in case a motherfucker wanna try you."

She laughed and tucked the gun into her purse.

* * *

Black bonded Cato out and as soon as Cato got access to a phone, he called Black. They met up at Spondivits to talk over lobster and beer.

"I appreciate what you did for me, bruh, and if there is anything I can do for you, just ask, bruh."

Black drank his beer and his mind went back to L. He remembered L's loyalty to him. He almost felt bad that he'd blamed everything on L, but he knew that L was looking down on him. He knew L wouldn't give a fuck. He was dead.

Cato cracked his lobster tails and said, "What are you thinking about, bruh?"

"About my man, L."

"L?"

"My friend. He was murdered and I didn't appreciate him until now when it's too late."

"That's the way it goes sometimes." Cato drank his beer but then said, "Black, I swear to God. I'm thankful for what you did and if you need me to handle anything, and I mean anything, I'm here for you, man. You feel me?" He tapped Black on the chest.

Black said, "As a matter of fact, there is a couple of things I want you to help me with."

"What?"

"I need you to…um…make a couple of dudes disappear. You know what I mean?"

"Just tell me who they are, I'll handle it. You feel me?"

"I believe you."

"How can I find them? You know where they are at?"

"I don't know where they are at. I don't even know how they look."

Cato dipped his lobster in butter sauce, gulped down some beer and let out a big burp. "I don't understand, bruh. How can I find them, if you don't even know where they're at?"

"There is a stripper named Sapphire. She works at Folleys. She's fucking one of them."

"Sapphire?"

"Yeah, she's a bad bitch. Seriously."

"But she ain't going to tell me about the nigga she fucking?"

"Maybe...maybe not."

Chapter 11

THE DJ CALLED SAPPHIRE UP TO THE STAGE. WHEN SHE walked on the stage, the bitch looked even more gorgeous that Cato imagined. She had the tiniest waist and some of the best natural titties he'd ever seen in his life. He could do without the tattoos, but he would absolutely fuck her.

Cato approached the stage and Sapphire backed that big ass up to the edge of the stage. She was wearing a blue G-string with rhinestones. He slapped her ass and threw a fistful of bills onto the stage then disappeared to find the waitress. He got five hundred more and he approached the stage again.

This time Sapphire pulled her panties aside and revealed a sapphire stone piercing her clit. Her pussy looked remarkable. Nice, clean, shaven, He hadn't had sex in six months and if he could, he would have fucked her right there on stage.

She turned to face him, tossed her hair and flashed a beautiful smile. Cato was still standing at the edge of the stage in awe of her. He was looking very thirsty and she laughed because it was amusing to her. She hugged him and he could smell her Bond Number 9 perfume.

"Thank you, baby," she said.

"Hey, I'm sitting over there in the corner. Come over and kick it with me when you get off stage."

She smiled and said, "I have to be on the center stage for the next song." She pointed to another stage across the room. "But as soon as I'm done over there, I'm all yours, baby."

"I like the sound of that," Cato said, then made a beeline to the table and ordered two bottles of Grey Goose. He put the bottles and a pile of cash on the table.

Two strippers, one short and one tall, approached. The tall one had a blue weave and blue contacts. She had decent-sized tits with no sag and nice hips, but no ass. The short one had long natural hair and lighter skin. She had silicone ass shots and tits like a twelve year old.

Cato wasn't impressed with either of them and he wished that they would just move the fuck on, but he knew they weren't going anywhere. Their thirsty asses had spotted the liquor and money. Blue hair plopped her ass right on his lap and he pushed her away.

"Scared of pussy?"

"Look, I don't like people sitting on my lap without asking."

The short girl said, "Why are you so angry, man? I mean all these beautiful girls in here and you mad?"

"I'm here to see somebody."

"Who?"

Blue hair said, "I saw his petty ass up there giving Sapphire a few coins. And when I say few, I do mean a few. I think he might have thrown twenty dollars at her and thought he was balling."

"Can I throw twenty dollars at you two birds so you can get the fuck away from me?"

"Yo baby mama a bird."

Blue hair approached him and Cato stood up. The tall bitch was actually looking down on him. He generally didn't fight girls but he had an assault on a female charge on his arrest record because one of his baby mama's had thrown a hot iron at him and it burned the back of his ankle. He'd beat her ass unconscious, in response. The police showed up and he tried to explain his side of the story, but they locked his ass up anyway. He didn't like fighting girls, but if this bitch thinks she's going to hit and he ain't going to knock the shit out of her, she had another thing coming.

She stood over him and he could smell the Trident gum that she was chewing like it was her last. "Motherfucker, you disrespect me, I will fuck you up in here."

"Get out of my face. You're the one that came over here fucking with me."

A humungous-ass, bearded, light-skinned man trotted up and said, "What the hell is going on?"

The short girl, who had been quiet, now said. "Kick this disrespectful motherfucker out."

The bouncer yanked Cato's arm and said, "Time to go, partna."

"Time to go my ass, and get yo motherfuckin' hands off me. Where the fuck is the owner? I done bought two bottles in this bitch. I ain't going no motherfuckin' where."

Seconds later, Sapphire appeared and wedged herself between the bouncer and Cato. She said to the bouncer, "He's one of my regular customers." She passed the bouncer a hundred dollar bill and said, "It's okay. He was waiting on me."

The bouncer turned to Cato and said, "I'm sorry for touching you."

The two men shook hands. "It's all good. You feel me?" Cato said.

The two strippers that he'd been arguing with were pissed, and they stormed away.

He sat back down and Sapphire sat down on his lap with her hands on his chest. He grabbed her ass and said, "I'm Cato."

• • •

His hands were bound by a rope tied to the bed rail. Blindfolded, his pale, white ass was exposed and snot cascaded from his nose into his mouth. He's just finished doing a few lines of coke. Miss America was spanking him with a wooden paddle and yelling, "You punk motherfucker! I need you to call me Master!"

"Master!" he yelled.

"Who's your daddy?"

"You are, daddy."

"Who's your mommy?"

"You are! You're my mommy and my daddy."

She untied him, situated a leash around his neck and paraded him around the room like he was a puppy. Commanding him to sit and stand, he obeyed most of the time and when he didn't obey, she slapped his pale, white ass with the paddle. The last few months, Craig had delved deeper into the world of BDSM. He thought he was a dominant person, but he discovered that he liked to be submissive as well. Dominating the women, but submitting to the trannies. He never let them penetrate him, but he liked to be tied up and he liked to be subservient to them. It just made him feel totally free.

After his session, Fy-Head visited and they all settled into the kitchen to converse over a bottle of Moscato, and of course, there was the eight ball of pure cocaine that he'd purchased from a biker earlier in the day.

Fy-Head said, "I know somebody that will do what you wanted. A professional."

"Who is it?" He folded a playing card and scooped some coke from the table and snorted.

"They don't want to meet you. In fact, they don't want to meet anybody."

His nose was running and they avoided making eye contact with him.

"So how is this going to work?"

"You give me the money and instructions on the job," Fy-head said as she sipped her Moscato. She poured another glass. "Give me her whereabouts and her routine. I relay all the info back to him and he watches her movements. He follows her and he completes the job."

"And I pay him when it's done?"

"Wrong."

"Half of the cash up front and the rest when the job is done?" Craig asked.

"No. He wants all his money first."

"I don't know, y'all. How do I know the job is going to get done?"

"It's a chance you have to take."

"Before I give you all of the money, I need to know your address."

"That's fine. We can go to my place right now if you want to go."

"Not right now. I'm going to need to know where your mother lives too."

"Look, I'll show you all of that. When do you want it done?"

"As soon as possible. Come by later and I'll give you the money."

"Give it to me now."

"I have to perform a procedure and I'll have it."

Fy-head said, "How much can you give me a new butt for?"

"If this goes right, I'll throw that in for free."

Fy-head stood, started twirling and said, "Ass gonna be on fleek."

They all laughed.

•   •   •

In the front of the studio, Brooke was watching Game of Thrones on her iPad when a young man entered the store. She looked up from her iPad. "Can I help you?"

He smiled. "In more ways than you can imagine, shawty." He smiled revealing a classless gold grill. Then he said, "Damn, you fine, shawty." He gave her a once over.

Brooke's black leggings made her legs look extra long and her butt pronounced. The young man was staring right at her ass to let her know that he absolutely approved of the outfit. He wasn't bad looking. Not as tall as she liked but she liked his smooth chocolaty skin and the way he dressed. He was wearing Jordan's and some fly red white and blue designer socks. True Religion shorts.

"What yo name is, shawty?"

"What's my name?"

"You ain't understand me?"

Brooke wanted to tell him she barely understood him but

she was sure this would insult him. "I'm Brooke."

"I'm DeMontre. My auntie own this place. Treat me right and I'll see if I can get her to get you a pay raise."

Brooke laughed and said, "Whatever."

"You got a man in yo life?"

"I got a boyfriend."

"I ain't say no boyfriend. You need a man."

"I supposed that man is you?"

"Damn, shawty, you smart."

"I wish you would quit calling me shawty."

"Oh, so you one of the bourgeoisie chicks, huh?"

Brooked scoffed and said, "Why do you say that?'

"I can tell. Talking all proper and shit. 'What makes you say that?'" He mocked her and laughed. "What school you go to?"

"What school do I attend?"

He laughed and said, "Yes. What school do you attend? Can you pass me the Grey Poupon?" he said, mocking her with an English accent. He was teasing her but she found this little bad boy fun.

She found herself laughing at him then she said, "I attend Atlanta Country Day. I only go twice a week, I'm a senior."

"Oh, I went to Booker T. Washington."

"You graduated?"

"I guess you can say that?"

He was staring at her ass and she liked that he liked it. At that moment, she could care less about her boyfriend. "What do you mean?"

"School wasn't for me, shawty. It was a waste of time."

"You weren't any good at it?"

"Look, shawty, I slept in school all day and I still took advanced classes and never made less than a B. Ask my auntie, she'll tell you."

Brooke had known boys like him. Some attended her school on a basketball scholarship and they were naturally smart but just didn't like school.

"Can we cut the school talk and talk about me taking you out?"

"You have a car?"

"Nope, but I can get one. "

Starr barged into the showroom and said to Brooke, "I see you met my nephew."

"Yeah."

DeMontre said, "Dang, auntie, why you ain't tell me your employee was so fine?"

Brooke was smiling hard as hell.

"Look, boy, don't you be harassing Brooke." Starr laughed and said, "What brings you up here?"

Seconds later Q entered the showroom and tossed DeMontre a set of keys.

Starr said, "What's going on in here?

"Uncle Q said I can wash the Range."

"What Range?"

"My Range Rover. I had my cars shipped up here."

"Oh," Starr said, "DeMontre, I ain't know you had a license?"

"Auntie, how you gonna try and play me like that?" He removed his license from his wallet and said, "I got Ls. I been had mine."

"Okay, boy, you're seventeen. How you going to say you been had yours?"

"I got them soon as I could get them. Come on, auntie, don't be a hater."

Q said, "Yeah, auntie, stop hating."

DeMontre inched toward the door and said, "Auntie, can shawty go with me?"

"No. She's working."

DeMontre looked at Brooke and said, "Shawty, I tried to get you off. Maybe next time."

Starr said to Q, "So how are you going to get home?"

"I'm staying here with you."

"Is that so?"

"Yeah."

"I've got paperwork to do."

"I'll help you," he said as he trailed her to the office.

Chapter 12

SAPPHIRE WAS ON TOP OF CATO RIDING HIM WHEN HE
said, "Lay on your stomach."

"What you going to do?"

"Just lay on your stomach."

"I hate anal."

"No anal. I promise."

She lay on her stomach and he gave her ass a massage with gels that he purchased from an adult toy store.

Cato grinned, studying that ginormous ass of hers as he applied oil and massaged the cheeks. Sapphire was not trying to get away but she couldn't stop squirming because it felt so damn good.

"How did you know, daddy?"

"How did I know what?"

"How did you know this was my hot spot?"

"Good guess?"

She laughed and said, "Great guess."

He then applied KY gel in her ass crack. This time she squirmed and tried to escape from his grip.

"I told you no anal."

"Look, it's not going to hurt, I promise. Plus, I'll give you fifteen hundred instead of a thousand."

"Where is the extra five hundred?"

"Do you think I would give you a thousand dollars and not give you the extra five hundred? Do I look like a petty-ass nigga?"

She laughed and said, "No."

"Relax, and I'm going to put it in slowly."

When she was fully relaxed, he eased the tip of penis into her tight asshole. She tensed up a bit but he gave her a back rub so she started to relax again. He pushed his dick further into her tight ass and as he thrusted slowly, she found it arousing. Her inner thighs moistened.

"Daddy, you were right. This shit is turning me on."

"I told you."

And he was turned on too. He loved anal more than he loved regular sex. It was about power to him and right now he was the man in charge.

"Harder!" she screamed.

He thrusted harder and she moaned, "Oh my god! This feels so good."

Seconds later, he placed the tip of a knife blade against her neck underneath her chin.

"If you scream, I will slit your throat, bitch."

"Oh my God! What's going on? Don't kill me. What do you want me to do? Suck your balls? I'll do anything that you ask!"

He slowly removed his dick from her ass crack and he stood her up with the knife blade still pressed against her neck. She was about to say something and he ordered her to shut the fuck up.

"I don't understand—"

With one swift move he lowered the knife and poked her ass cheek. Blood discharged from her ass. "Next time, it's in your asshole. I swear to God. Do you understand me?"

He stood behind her. His arm enveloped her tiny neck. "I need you to tell me who the fuck is after my boy?'

"Who is your boy?"

"Black."

"Black who?"

"Oh, now you want to play dumb?" He released her before he gathered his boxer shorts and slid into them.

"So you're trying to tell me that you don't know him?"

"I'm not saying that. I know a lot of guys name Black. Be specific."

"I'm talking about the motherfucker that you been discussing with some Detroit niggas."

She stood there butt ass naked trying to think of what she was going to do. She knew that if she told this nigga where they were and something happened to them, she would surely die. But if she didn't tell him something, she was going to surely die. She hesitated then asked, "Can I put my clothes on?"

"You can put your panties on and some shorts and a T-shirt. No shoes." He didn't want her wearing shoes to prevent her from running. But if she did run, he had a .45 automatic and he wouldn't hesitate to blast her in the back.

She slid into a pink Victoria Secret short set.

"Now, tell me about the Detroit boys."

"Well, the one that I knew about was Todd." Todd wasn't from Detroit but he was a safe option.

"How do you know him?"

"I met him in the club a few years back. He came in and we sat and talked. He told me he worked for a madam. Told me that she wanted him to recruit some pretty girls. Told me I could make up to ten grand a night, but I would have to split it with the madam. I told him to sign me up, but he told me that first he would have to fuck me to test me out and see if I was worth it. I fucked him and then he took pictures of me back to this so-called madam who then said I was too thick for her clientele. Said that her clients liked skinny bitches and as you can see, I ain't hardly no skinny bitch. I'm Georgia born and raised."

"Y'all exchanged numbers?"

"Yeah, I got it."

"Perfect. Need you to call him over. Call him now."

Her iPhone was on the nightstand. She inched her way over to the stand while she kept her eye on him. Thinking just a few minutes ago, he was giving her some incredible anal, now he was threatening to kill her. She dialed Todd's number.

"Hello?"

"Todd, can you come over? I need to tell you something."

"I'm kind of busy right now. What do you need?"

"It's important."

"Look, I can't come. I'm busy. I'll catch up with you tomorrow." Todd then hung up the phone.

"Do you know where he lives?" Cato asked Sapphire.

"I don't."

"Come here."

She eased her way over. He ripped her Victoria Secret shorts off.

She said, "What the fuck are you doing?"

"Give me your phone and spread your goddamned legs."

She obliged. He took six pictures of her with her pussy spread and one of that little tight asshole that he had just enjoyed. He then told her to stand up and let her get dressed. She put on another short set that was identical to the one Cato had just ripped off except that this one was sky blue.

"Now I need you to send all six of those pictures to Todd."

She did and seconds later, Todd called.

"What the fuck are you doing?"

"Look, I need you tonight."

"I don't have no money and I know you ain't fucking me for free."

"I'm horny, Todd. I don't need no money right now. Just come over. "

"You still live at the same place?"

"Yeah."

"Text me the address. And I'll be over in a few hours."

Chapter 13

ASIA WAS STANDING OUTSIDE WHEN BLACK WHIPPED the rental car into Asia's driveway. He was supposed to be in jail. How did he get out? "You made bond?"

"Yes."

She led him inside the house then offered him a seat.

"No, that's okay," Black said.

"The kids are not here."

"That's okay."

She took a deep breath and waited on him to speak. "I know you called the police on me."

"I didn't have a choice."

"There's always a choice."

She turned away from him, tugging at her ear trying to decide if she was going to tell him the truth. "Two black detectives came over and asked did you have my car. I told them I hadn't seen you and then they showed me a text message exchange between me and you and I had no choice. They knew everything."

He stood there and took it all in. He knew she was right. She didn't have a choice. "Look, I'm not mad. You had to do what you had to do. But why did you have to tell them when

I was coming?" He paused then he decided that he would take a seat after all. He sat in a chair in the corner of the living room.

"I know it was wrong."

"You damn right it was wrong. I got locked up right there in front of my kids. "

Tears formed in Asia's eyes. "Black, it's not like you're the best dad."

"What? I was taking them to the movies."

"Black, they hardly see you. And I was at Nana's house a few weeks ago and ran into your other baby mama?"

"Which one?"

"Shakira."

Shakira was Black's oldest son Dion's mother. Dion was fifteen.

"Oh that bitch. What did she have to say?"

"Says you haven't seen your son in months. So I guess I'm lucky that my kids get to see you."

Black listened. He knew what she was saying was right but he had his reasons. He didn't care for Shakira and he'd almost got into a fight with her new man, so in his mind he had good reasons for his negligence. He'd lost the love of his life and people were out to kill him. He didn't want to risk putting his kids in jeopardy. He couldn't stay away from Tierany and Man-Man too long because they were his youngest.

"Have you seen any of the others?" Asia asked.

"No," Black said then paused. "Your point?"

"My point is that you used to be a good dad and that's the one thing me and all of your other kids' mothers could agree on. Not only did you give them money, but you used to be there for them. You know how many times I have to hear Man-Man say, 'Is my daddy going to come to my game?' or Tierany ask if you're going to see her gymnastics performance? And I have to say that you have to work."

"What are you saying?"

"You're not a dad. Not a dad that I can be proud of anymore. You've got shot twice. You're going to jail every other week. What the fuck? How can you look in the mirror and call yourself a good man?"

"I never said that." Black stood and said, "You're just trying to justify the foul shit you did."

"I did what I did. Yeah, I kinda wanted you to go to jail because I'd rather tell the kids that you are in prison than dead."

Black stood there pondering. His phone buzzed. A text from TeTe. He would read it later. He knew what Asia was saying was absolutely right. But his plan was to get next to the connect, open even more Wing Kings and go one hundred percent legit if he could. But he knew that he'd have to find something else that would give him that rush. He knew he was sick because he felt a high that he couldn't explain—not from doing drugs, but from getting away with illegal shit. He loved being the bad guy. It was a role that he would miss.

"Look, I'm going to be a better father."

"Be a better person, Black. God has blessed you with wonderful children and a family that cares about you. And you are about to throw it all away. And who was that crazy bitch you brought to my house? Something is not right with that woman."

Black laughed and said, "You tripping."

Asia said, "I ain't gonna lie. That old bitch was fly but she looked crazy, like she'll cut your dick off crazy."

Black was laughing his ass off because he knew that TeTe would indeed cut your dick off.

Chapter 14

CATO WIPED HIS MOUTH WITH A PAPER TOWEL AFTER finishing the grilled ham and cheese sandwich that he'd ordered Sapphire to prepare for him.

"Come here, bitch."

She moseyed that big ass of hers over in his direction. When she was face to face with him, he removed his penis from his pants. Though he was a short man, he had a huge penis. Thick, chocolate and veiny. The women loved it. He ordered her on her knees.

"Todd will be here in a second. "

"You said that twenty minutes ago." He brandished the knife and placed the cold steel against her neck and said, "Get your ass on your knees."

Seconds later, she was down on her knees with her mouth wide open. He placed that blade right against her cheek and said, "If you bite me, I swear to God I will slash your goddamned pretty face."

She deep throated him, thinking that he must have read her mind because she had thought about biting the fuck out of him. But she knew he had weapons. Instead, she did exactly as he'd told her. His balls smelled like musty armpits and she wanted to gag. She would suck and suck and every three minutes she would pause to get some air.

When she stopped for air, he said, "We don't take breaks around here. Get back to work."

Why wasn't he cumming, Sapphire thought. He hadn't showered from the anal sex that they'd had earlier, but luckily they used a condom, otherwise she'd really be disgusted.

She stopped and he frowned but before he could say it, she said it for him, "I know, we don't take breaks around here."

He smiled. "You're learning."

"My jaw hurts."

"Your fucking neck is going to be hurting if you don't get back to work."

"Why won't you cum? What is wrong with you?"

Now she was pissing him off. He poked her in her pretty little face with the blade. He didn't cut her, but she knew that he would, so she started sucking as hard as she could. Spit and vacuum sounds filled the room. He smiled, and minutes later, he came hard. Semen travelled down the side of her mouth and she smiled. Although this was totally against her will, she still took a sick delight in pleasing him. She stood and began to make a beeline to the restroom.

"Where are you going?" Cato asked.

She opened her mouth revealing the ocean of semen and pointed to let him know that she wanted to spit it out.

"We swallow around here."

She made a sad face. He poked her in the leg with the knife, piercing her skin and he said, "Open your mouth."

She opened her mouth again.

"Swallow like a good little girl."

She gulped down his sour, disgusting semen. She could only imagine what his diet was like.

The doorbell chimed and he struggled to zip up his pants. He removed the gun from his waistband and hid behind the door.

Sapphire said, "Who is it?"

"Todd."

Cato whispered a script for her to repeat.

"Wait a minute, Todd. Let me slip into some clothes."

Todd said, "Stay naked."

Cato stood still behind the door, being as quiet as he possibly could. His gun cocked and she opened the door.

Todd said, "What's up, baby! Why are you wearing clothes?"

Cato was thinking of the things that he was going to do to this bitch ass nigga. He would strip him of his clothes. Burn him with the iron. Sprinkle hot grease on his balls. Pull his pubic hair out and douse him with alcohol. He would make this bitch pay before he decided to kill him and he would have to kill her too. He couldn't leave any witnesses.

She peeled out of the bathrobe and Todd said, "You know I'm a sucker for your body. Why are you doing this to me?"

When Cato could just see Todd, he kicked the door shut. He was surprised when he and Todd were face to face and he realized Todd was holding a gun, but he didn't flinch; instead, he fired. Nothing came out. His gun had jammed. He didn't have time to figure out what the fuck was going on; instead, he lunged forward at Todd. Todd fired two shots into Cato's head, He collapsed onto the wall, his brains spilling from his head. Cato died immediately.

She said, "Damn, I'm so glad you came."

"Well, when I got your 911 text with the pictures, I knew you were in trouble."

"Thank you. You saved my life."

"I read the 911 text."

"Yeah I'm surprised the stupid motherfucker didn't ask to see my phone."

He cleaned the gun up and passed it to her. "Tell the police that he tried to break in and you shot him."

"But his DNA is in the bedroom and even inside of me."

"You fucked him?"

"We were tricking."

"Well, tell them that you fucked him and he left and came back with a gun and tried to force himself on you at gunpoint. You had to kill him. Your phone in your name?"

"No."

"Good, give it to me. You call them from a neighbor's house."

"Okay, I will."

He hugged her and said, "I'll bring your phone back in a week. Or call me when you get another phone."

Chapter 15

CHANEL WAS WEARING A LITTLE, TIGHT, BACKLESS DRESS
that clung to her perfect body when Q picked her up in his
Range Rover. He really didn't know her and he didn't want
her to know what he did or exactly what kind of money he
could get his hands on. She lived in some condo near Lennox
mall.

He watched her pretty ass as she strolled to the car. When
she finally made it to the car, he hopped out and opened the
door for her.

She hopped inside the car and he greeted her with a hug.

"Nice ride," she said.

"Thanks."

"I have a white one."

He glanced over at her. He wasn't surprised. Everybody in
Atlanta seemed to be driving Range Rovers. But he knew
that most of them couldn't afford them. He knew she could
probably afford hers though. She made it clear that she
liked nice things and that she was willing to work for them.
Plus she had made it clear that she was a woman of high
expectations. He didn't know if that was a good thing or
not. The Geto Boys were playing on his Pandora Station.

"What's that on the radio?"

"Geto Boys. You ever heard of them?"

"Yeah."

"Scarface Station on Pandora."

"My Uncle Ray liked Scarface. Can you put it on something else? That's kind of old school."

"What you wanna listen to, Ms. Chanel?"

"I don't know. Meek Mills, Kendrick Lamar, ASAP Rocky, you know, anything more up to date. I don't like old stuff."

"Damn, I'm glad you told me that. I was thinking about picking you up in my old pickup truck."

"Then we would have rode in separate cars."

"Are you serious?"

"I am serious. I don't like old cars, old homes or old clothes."

"And old rap artists."

"Exactly."

"Well, I'm ten years older than you, at least."

"It's okay. I like older guys."

"Why do you think you like older guys?"

Q was zooming up Peachtree and they were listening to Rhianna's Bitch Better Have My Money.

She said, "Older men know what they want. Well, most of them. Guys my age don't have their shit together and most aren't as ambitious as I am. I'm looking for a husband and I haven't met anybody on my level."

"Oh yeah?"

"Not in Atlanta."

"What about the guy that you had been dating?"

She looked startled and she actually turned away from his glance and looked pensively out the window. "How did you know I was dating someone?"

"You told me."

"I told you that?" She seemed to be trying to remember when she told him. She didn't remember telling him anything like that.

"Well, you said that everyone has someone."

"You're right. I remember now." She laughed revealing a perfect smile. He could tell Chanel was the kind of girl that got her teeth whitened regularly. She seemed very vain, but it didn't bother him too much because he liked a woman that took pride in her looks.

"Tell me about him."

"Only if you tell me about her."

"What do you want to know about her?"

"Where does she live?"

"Atlanta."

"What don't you like about her?"

"I like everything about her."

"So why ain't you with her?" She paused and said, "Or are you with her?"

"If I was with her, I wouldn't be here."

"I don't know. You know how these Atlanta guys are."

"I ain't from Atlanta."

"Well, what's the deal, Q? Why ain't you with your girl?"

He sighed and said, "She's on the insecure side."

"Is she overweight?"

"No, she's gorgeous."

Now he was pissing Chanel off. What the fuck was he here with her for claiming that another bitch was gorgeous? She would not let on that this was bothering her though. She turned to him and said, "So what did you do, Q?"

"What made you think I did something?"

"I mean someone made her insecure. Did you cheat on her with some exotic girl? You know how dudes are nowadays. How they want something exotic. Is that what you want, Q? Some exotic girl? Some foreign girl? Black girls aren't good enough anymore?"

"No. Nothing like that. It's all on her. Her ex dogged her out pretty bad and had a baby on her."

"How you know what she's telling you is true?"

"Me and her ex were friends."

"And you took that man's girl? What the fuck?" She looked disgusted.

"No, he was murdered."

"Oh."

"So, if she didn't want a break, you would be with her?"

"Maybe."

Moments later, they arrived at RA sushi and they were seated in a booth up near the entrance. She ordered the spicy tuna roll. He decided not to eat.

"So you're not eating?" she asked.

He said, "Only niggas trying to be bourgeoisie eat this shit."

She laughed and said, "People say that I'm bourgeoisie."

"What would you say?"

She smiled and said, "Maybe." She sipped her water and then said, "Do you still like me?"

"Of course."

She blushed and she had to admit that she liked him too. There were qualities about him that told her he was a very sophisticated man whether he wanted to admit it or not. He reminded her that he'd grown up poor and she was almost certain that he was the type of man that could handle a girl like her.

After they left the restaurant, he felt a buzz and she was looking great to him. He reached over and rubbed her leg but she stopped him.

"Look, I like you, but I don't want to do it just yet. I'm not some one night stand."

He smiled and said, "Well, if it makes you feel any better, we can do it tomorrow too."

She laughed at his brashness. She wanted him as much as he wanted her, but she could tell that he was in love with this other woman. She knew that they could be a power couple but she had to guard her heart.

When he pulled up in front of her home, he leaned forward and said, "I like you, Chanel."

"You like me? How do you know that?"

"What do you mean? How do I know that?"

"How does anyone know if they like someone? I mean, sometimes men get caught up in the outer appearance. They don't take time to get to know me and when they do get to know me, they realize I'm a lot to handle."

Q knew she was a lot to handle. He had been with women like her before. She was the kind of girl that wouldn't eat at a local steakhouse. She needed designer things, which meant that she was a little insecure, but so was he. At least he knew what to expect.

He said, "I know more about you than you think."
"What is that supposed to mean?"
"Let's just go with the flow."
"Let's do that."
He leaned into her and kissed her. The taste of her tongue reminded him of peaches but what else would you expect from a girl like Chanel?

Chapter 16

HIS NAME WAS MAYOR PHIL ANDERSON. HE LIKED expensive suits and expensive cars. He liked the forbidden. He was fifty-four and the mayor of one of the most electrifying cites in the U.S. It was a place where the influencers of the south wanted to be. A city full of athletes, entertainers, and international businessmen that were willing to pay for favors, and he was willing to give it to them if the price was right. He'd made a small fortune selling favors.

As soon as this term was over, he would take a year off and travel the world and maybe run for governor. He wasn't passionate about politics, but he loved the power and he loved the benefits. Especially here in Atlanta. It was nothing for a celebrity to send him an envelope full of cash in exchange for a small favor or send over some strippers to keep him entertained. Drug dealers would send cash for him to use his influence to get the police chief to keep the heat off their asses—at least the ones that played the game.

But there was one drug dealer that he had to eliminate. He was getting too close for comfort and had too much influence over his daughter. He'd learned about him months ago when he had a P.I. tail Sasha. The P.I. witnessed a meeting with Sasha, a woman named Rashida and Tyrann Massey, a.k.a. Black. The P.I. came back saying that Black was a known drug dealer and was suspected of selling heroin; the same heroin that he had declared war on during a press conference months ago. The heroin was off the street and Black had gotten arrested but someone else had taken the fall for him.

For the past few days, the mayor had tried to contact Sasha, but she'd avoided him and so now he decided that he would show up at her home to see what was going on. He took a swig of Grand Marnier before tiptoeing into her condo. He found her sitting Indian style on her sofa typing on her MacBook Air.

She looked up from her computer. They made eye contact as he barged right into the kitchen and grabbed a bottle of alkaline water from the fridge. Fancy water in a fancy bottle, he thought. A waste of goddamned money if you asked him. Her eyeballs trailed him as he unscrewed the top off the water. He sat across from her on an armchair.

He sipped his water and said, "You haven't answered my calls."

She kept pecking away on her laptop without answering or looking up at him.

"I know you hear me."

"I do."

"Okay. What the fuck is wrong with you?"

She sat the laptop down and said, "No, what the fuck is wrong with you?"

"It's that dope dealer friend of yours."

"What are you talking about?"

"You didn't think I knew about him, huh?"

"Actually, I don't care if you know about him or not. I can do whatever I want to. I'm tired of you trying to control me. I don't want to be controlled. Look, I know I work for you but you don't own me."

The mayor set the water down on the table and looked at her. "Where is all this resentment coming from? I've been nothing but good to you. I sent you to the best schools. I've given you your job and this is how you thank me? By being rude to me?"

"Please." Her eyes sparked with anger. "What part of, 'You can't control me' don't you understand?"

"I've never tried to control you."

He made his way over to her. She set the MacBook Air down and stood up. He grabbed her arms and she said, "You get away from me. I'll scream. I swear if you touch me, I will scream."

He grabbed her arms and she screamed for a second before he used his hands to muffle the sound. She stumbled back on the sofa with him still on top of her, his hand cuffing her mouth.

"You ungrateful hussy." He removed his hand and replaced it with his mouth. He kissed her like he'd done so many times before. He attempted to remove her shirt. The usual routine was that he'd remove her bra, play with her nipples and then spank her ass or lick her VJ. The first time he'd licked her VJ was when she was eight years old, before she'd heard anything about sex. All she knew was that Daddy made her feel good when he did that and she thought it was normal. But he would always tell her not to tell anybody. Not even mommy. This went on for years, until one day she learned the word molestation and found out that what Daddy was doing was wrong. She felt disgusted and ever since that day, she felt unworthy of love. So she did all she could to block these deeds out of her mind.

She went to the best schools in Atlanta and excelled academically and athletically. She graduated high school as salutatorian and was offered scholarships from a number of schools. She'd applied to and been accepted into Emory University but there wasn't a scholarship offer so her father had paid her tuition in full.

He was still tugging at her shirt and she screamed, "Get off me! Get off me!"

His breath smelled of Grand Marnier. He stepped back. "You think he's going to do for you what I've been doing for you?"

"You mean what you been doing to me? Is that what you mean?"

"Look, I never thought I'd see the day—"

"That I'd resist your advances."

He inched toward her and she backpedaled.

"You don't love me." he said.

Their eyes met for a brief moment. "I never have."

"You loved me and I loved you. It's been that way since you were a little girl. We've always been there for each other. Just me and you. We've never let anybody get in between us." Tears welled in his eyes. "Don't turn your back on me. I need you. I really need you," he pleaded.

She dashed into the bedroom. He removed another mini bottle of Grand Marnier from his pocket and downed it with one drink before following her. She knew there was a snubnosed .38 on the nightstand. She opened the drawer and removed it then pointed it at him.

He halted and said, "What is this about?"

"Look, you don't have to worry 'bout me saying shit about your dealings. I just want you out of my life."

"If you think that you're going to have a happy ever after with your boyfriend, you're wrong. The Feds are on his ass and it's just a matter of time before they get him."

"Get the fuck out of my house!" she shouted.

"What about my money?"

"What money?"

"Oh, don't play stupid, bitch."

"What money are you talking about?"

"I'm talking about the money that I had you put in the Panama accounts. I need that money if you ever want me out of your life."

"I'll give you the money."

He took a step toward her and she was shaking like hell. She knew that if she pulled that trigger, it would end all of her worries. She contemplated it but before she could decide what to do, he knocked the gun out of her hand and it fell on the floor.

He approached her and placed his hand around her neck. "You're a dumb little bitch and you always will be a dumb bitch. Look, I need my money. So you best hop a plane over to Panama City to get my money."

"If I don't?"

"My people are coming for you and I don't have to tell you who they are, do I? Play with me, bitch, and you will die. I promise you."

He made his way through the bedroom door. Then, he removed yet another bottle of Grand Marnier from his pocket and downed it before slinging the bottle against the wall and shattering it into pieces.

Chapter 17

TETE HAD HIRED A DRIVER FOR THE NIGHT BECAUSE SHE
knew there would be lots of fun and drinks. This was the first
night that she'd been out with Black on a date since he got
out of jail. She and Black sat in the back of the stretch Rolls
Royce. She was wearing a royal blue dress that shellacked
her body and looked incredible against her skin. It made
her look curvier than she actually was and the fragrance
of the night was Bvlgari Rose Essentielle. And just as she
suspected, Black couldn't keep his hands off her. He yanked
her panties down in the backseat and she slid them into her
purse. He jammed his fingers into her VJ and she moaned.
Black was sure that the driver heard as he noticed the driver
glancing in the mirror. TeTe's moaning was deafening.
Black tried to cover her mouth with his free hand and she
lashed out at him.

"What the fuck are you doing?"

"He's going to hear us."

"I do whatever the fuck I wanna do. He works for me. He
seen all kinds of shit, I'm sure."

There was a wet bar in the back of the ride and she poured
herself a shot of Patron, sipped it and then freed Black's

manhood from his pants. She dropped down and stuck it in her mouth.

Black was hesitant, as he saw the driver glance in the mirror. This time, the man smiled, embarrassed that he had been so goddamned nosey.

"Do you want to listen to some music?" the driver asked.

"Yeah. Trap music."

Fuck Up Some Commas by Future blasted through the speakers. Black downed a shot of Patron then he relaxed. Her fingers were gripping his balls and she was slurping the tip of his penis. He was hypersensitive because he hadn't had sex in two weeks and although he didn't usually get this hard from head, right now, his dick was hard enough to knock a dent in a car door. Every time she was about to bring him to an orgasm, he would grab her hair and she would look up at him, saliva cascading down the side of her right jaw. She smiled because she knew that he was aroused and that she had done her job. She continued performing and he stopped her again.

"What's wrong?" she asked.

"Nothing," he lied but the truth was that he couldn't get relaxed. He hadn't heard from Cato and he was wondering what had happened with Avant.

She rose from his lap and she kissed him. "Something is bothering you."

"Is it that obvious?"

"Yes."

He zipped up his pants and asked the driver to lower the volume on the radio. He sighed and said, "The dude from my basement?"

"What about him?"

"How the fuck did he get out?"

"Is that what has you worried?"

"Yeah."

"I would have killed him."

He laughed and said, "I believe you."

"You think I'm a joke?"

"No."

The car stopped and they were at Halo. The driver lowered

the volume of the music and said, "We're at the Biltmore. There seems to be a nice crowd at Halo."

"Hey, just ride around the city." TeTe ordered."

"Joy riding?" the driver said.

"Well, joy riding would be if we stole the car."

The man laughed and said, "Poor word choice."

"We are just wandering aimlessly. We don't have no destination. The night is young and we're young. We are having fun," TeTe said. Although she wasn't exactly young, Black made her feel young and they were having fun.

The driver obliged and when they were exiting on to I-75 Black said, "I almost forgot to tell you."

Her face became serious. "You forgot to tell me what?"

"I heard in the streets that Todd is out to get me and you for what happened to his cousin. He actually met up with Shakur's brothers and told them that you masterminded the murder."

She unzipped his pants and said, "I don't care about Todd. I'm not worrying about him." She stroked his penis until it sprang to life and was pointing to the roof of the limo. She hopped up on top of him and straddled him as the limo darted across the overpass on I-75. The bright Atlanta skyline was in the background as music played on the radio.

Chapter 18

AFTER Q HAD RECEIVED A SHIPMENT FROM GORDO, HE drove over to Fresh's new home. Today was the first time he had seen Fresh's new place. He was impressed right away as Fresh gave him a tour.

Q said, "I love this place. How did you find it?"

"I love it too. A realtor found it."

As they settled down in the living room, Fresh offered Q a drink.

"Do you mind if I smoke?" Fresh asked.

"I thought you stopped?"

"Got a lot of shit on my mind."

"Light up."

Fresh rolled a swisher.

"What's on ya mind, big bro?" Fresh said as he inhaled the weed. He coughed and fanned the weed. The scent of the Bubba Kush annoyed the hell out of Q but he dealt with it.

"Chanel's a winner, right?" Fresh said.

"I like her a lot."

Fresh coughed, laughed and said, "I told you."

"You did."

"She told Brianna that she liked you, but she wasn't going

to open up to you too much because you were still in love with Starr."

Q turned from Fresh's gaze. "I do still love her."

"Look, man, don't miss out on something good chasing something temporary," Fresh said.

"Chanel is the one that might be temporary."

"Starr got you whipped."

"I am."

"Enough of the talk about the women. What's on your mind?"

"Big shipment from Gordo."

Fresh took a toke on the swisher and blew a smoke ring before coughing. Q wondered why in the fuck did he care so much about something that made him cough that much.

"I already got work."

"From who?"

"Diego."

"You did?"

"Yeah, bruh. You don't remember?" He paused before inhaling and blowing another smoke ring. "I'm the smoker and you're the one with the bad memory."

Q was fanning the smoke as if it bothered him and when Fresh noticed it, he stubbed it out and reached for a bottle of Effen that was on the table and drank it straight.

"I told you I was going to deal with him and you said we shouldn't, but then I said I was going to get back what he owed us. I'm going to get him, man. I told you all of that."

Q remembered, but he didn't actually believe Fresh would deal with him and though he was going to get back at Diego, he wanted it to be planned out—not some bullshit plan that Fresh drew in the dirt with a stick.

"Look, man, I met some people through my cousin and they are willing to help us out in any way."

"What cousin?"

"I have a cousin named Tommy. He lives here. He left Houston when he was nine and has been here ever since."

"Tommy deals? Funny I've never heard about him before."

"Tommy doesn't deal. He's into that music bullshit but all his friends are trappers, bruh."

Q was listening intently.

"Look, after I make enough money, I'm going to handle this dude for Rico and that's on everything I love. On my mama. I'm going to make that motherfucker pay."

"I don't want you to fuck with the dude. I want you to deal with me. We can get him later."

"You're my brother, Q, and I love you. I'm always down with you, but this is something I gotta do. I can't let this ride. I wanna handle this."

"There is a right way to do shit and this ain't it. We can't bring Rico back."

"I'm going to handle it right now." Fresh was annoyed at Q's rationalization and he lit another swisher. "You don't understand, Q. I'm going to bait him until he gives me a big load and I'm not going to pay him. Not only that, the dumb motherfucker showed me where he lives."

"Where he lives?"

"Yeah, he has a house in Atlanta."

"Really?"

"He's here, Q, and I'm going to take his shit and then kill him. I'm going to do it and I don't give a fuck what you say."

"Not a good idea."

"Tell me why?" Fresh said, the swisher dangling from his mouth.

Seconds later, a girl came from the bedroom—a woman that Q had never seen before. The woman was very curvaceous with natural hair and just a hint of eye shadow. She pranced around the house in a pair of pink booty shorts.

Fresh said, "Meet my new lady."

Q nodded to the woman. He was clearly pissed off that the woman was present. Fresh turned to her and said, "Look, baby, can you let me and my brother talk?"

She gave Fresh a peck on the jaw and said, "I'll be waiting."

Q and Fresh were quiet until after she had disappeared, Q said, "Okay, is this how we're doing business now? We come to Atlanta and lose our fucking minds?"

"Look, I don't know what you thinking, but I'm not your son." He stubbed the cigar out again and said, "You want out, remember?"

"Yes, I remember and you talked me back in. You begged me."

"Because they had Rico and you didn't give a fuck if he lived or died."

"I did everything they asked me to do and what did it get us? Rico was still murdered."

"And I'm going to make it right."

"You got bitches over while we're talking business."

"I didn't know you were going to show up at my house."

"You should have told me she was here."

"I wasn't thinking."

"You know why you wasn't thinking? Cuz you're a weed head."

Fresh took hold of Q's arm and attempted to lead him to the door when Q broke free from his grip and said, "Get the fuck off me, man! Don't touch me!"

"Get out of my house, man! Who the fuck are you to call me a weed head!"

Fresh marched right over and yanked the door open and Q walked right by him. Neither uttered a word.

Chapter 19

INSIDE A RUNDOWN SUPER 8 MOTEL IN ROOM ONE-OH-
six, Fy-head introduced Craig Matthews to J-Will. J-Will was
a bulky guy with a broad forehead and hair in a kinky twist.
He was wearing a tiny red superman shirt that struggled to
contain his big-ass stomach.

They exchanged handshakes and J-Will said to Craig, "Befo'
I discuss any motherfuckin' thang, I need you to strip."

Craig's nostrils flared. He was clearly mad but J-Will just
stood there with his hands on his waist waiting.

Fy-Head faked a smiled and said, "Jay don't mean no harm.
I mean he's just nervous. He did ten years in the pen and he
ain't trying to go back."

"I did fit-teen years and been in and out all my goddamned
life and I ain't trying to go back fuckin' with some bullshit-
ass cracka."

Craig laughed a little before peeling his clothes off and
kicking them in a corner. Soon, he stood butt-naked in the
room.

There was a six-pack of Bud light on the table and J-Will
offered Craig one when he saw he wasn't wearing a wire
and realized that it was okay to talk.

"No, thank you."

"Fy-Head said you needed a job done."

"Who?"

Cassandra laughed and said, "Fy-head a nickname of mine."

Craig laughed and said, "Yeah, I need a job done."

"Okay, tell me about it."

Craig said, "Now, wait a minute. You had me strip-searched to make sure I wasn't wired up. How do I know it's okay to talk around you?"

J-Will met Fy-Head's eyes and then he turned back to Craig and said, "Because it is, motherfucker. Either you play by my rules or you can get the fuck out of here. You need me. I don't need you." His nostrils flared.

"Have you done this sort of thing before?"

"Done what? You haven't told me what the fuck you want done."

"I need my wife dead."

"Okay, now we're talking."

"Can you do it?"

"I can kill anybody if you pay me the right amount of money."

"I don't like no sloppy jobs. Are you a professional?"

"What does a professional look like?"

"Not like you." Craig's eyes darted around the small hotel room. Then he turned to Fy- head who was sitting on the edge of the bed filing her nails. "How long have you known him?"

"We met on the inside."

"I thought you said you were a professional?"

"I ain't say a motherfucking thang. I asked you what does a professional look like."

Fy-head stood from the bed and said, "Can you cut all the questions out? You are making us nervous. I don't want to go to prison dealing with your scared ass."

J-Will opened his beer, downed it and burped.

Craig said, "Listen, I'm sorry for all the questions. I just wanna be safe."

J-Will grabbed a second can of beer and sat in a chair

that was behind the desk. "I'm going to need to know her schedule. The alarm code to the house. Is there cameras? What kind of security system do you have? Do you have a key or can you tell me where I can catch her? Does she work out at a gym? What are her hobbies? Who lives in her home? Are there kids there? If so, what do you want me to do with them?"

"Kids are there. I don't have the alarm code but I can call. The alarm is still in my name."

"Okay. I'm going to need a map of the house. Need to know what room is hers."

"I can get you a layout of the home."

"Good." He swallowed the beer in one drink and said, "Okay, how much you paying?"

"Fifteen grand."

"Where is the money?"

"I don't have it all."

Craig turned to Fy-head who was fixing her hair in the tiny cramped bathroom. Craig said, "I told Cassandra that I was going to give you half upfront and half after the job is done."

"Look, bruh, this is murder for hire. You ain't paying on a gold chain in the pawnshop. I don't do layaway plans."

"I don't understand."

"If you ain't got fifteen upfront and you want to pay half, then my price goes up to twenty thousand. Take it or leave it."

Craig turned to Fy-head. "I've got the money, but that's not the deal I discussed with you."

"She ain't the one doing the job. I'm doing the job. So you need to deal with me."

Craig had no choice. He had to take the deal. He'd just plotted a murder with a stranger. This would be one more person knowing about his plans.

Fy-head came back from the bathroom and Craig said to her, "I told you that we were going to do half upfront."

"Look, I told him. It's up to him. I'm not doing the job."

"The free surgery is off the table then."

J-Will said, "What's going on?"

Fy- head said," Our friend here is a plastic surgeon. He told me that if I found someone who would do the job, he would give me free ass implants. Now he's reneging since you want all your money."

"I do want all my money and he's going to perform the procedure or I'm not doing the goddamned job. You brought us two together and you deserve to be compensated."

Craig frowned. He couldn't believe that he'd just been bitched but there was nothing he could do about it. He removed the money and passed the money to J-Will who counted it and gave him a tiny flip phone.

"What's this?"

"This is the phone that I want you to communicate with me with."

"Text?"

"Not text."

"Why not?"

"It's written proof."

J-Will flashed his flip phone. "These lines are safe and I will keep you updated on the moves I make. I will let you know when the job is done."

"How will I find you?"

"I just gave you a phone and I gave you my number."

"But what if you don't do the job?"

"You don't have that to worry about. I'm six for six."

Chapter 20

"*DAT ASS THO, SHAWTY.*"
Brooke turned and looked and just as she thought, it was DeMontre standing there smiling and examining her ass, His gold teeth blinging, and he wore a fresh pair of Jordan's. He was the exact kind of guy her Mom had warned her about, but she had to admit that he was intriguing.

"So what kind of stuff you like to get into, shawty? What y'all be doing over there at that rich school?"

"All I do is work and play sports."

"You run track?" He laughed and said, "Let me guess. You look like you play lacrosse or some ole corny shit like that. Maybe cross country. I can't see you running track."

"What's wrong with that?"

"That ain't no black-person sport, shawty."

"Actually, I play tennis."

"Ok, that's better."

She chuckled. He was a typical hood dude, making fun of the way she talked.

"So when you gonna take me out?" DeMontre asked.

"Excuse me?"

"You heard me. When you gonna take me out?"

"You're the man. You're supposed to take me out."

"Yeah, but your folks caked up."

"I will not be taking no man out."

"Okay, when you gonna let me take you out?"

"That's more like it."

"So when are you gonna make it happen? I don't need my auntie all up in my business either, feel me?"

Oh my god, she thought. Shawty was bad but you feel me? She'd vowed that she'd never date anybody like that, but he was cute and she liked his sense of humor.

"You don't want your auntie in your business? I didn't say I was going out with you."

"What you waiting on?"

Those gold teeth were blinding her. "You don't even know if I have a boyfriend," she said.

"You already told me that you did. Now give me your phone."

"For what?"

"I'm going to put my number in it."

She hesitated and he snatched it out of her hand before she could deny him. He put his number in and typed Twin in the name column.

"Twin?"

"Yeah, I got a twin brother."

"Two of y'all?"

"You got a partna?"

"Maybe."

Starr appeared and said, "Stop harassing my employee, DeMontre."

"No. I was just paying her a couple of compliments. You know, for her proper etiquette."

"You might learn something from her. She's a smart girl. Not like them ratchet hood rats that you like."

"Auntie got jokes."

"So why are you here?"

"I'm 'pose to be meeting Q over here."

"Supposed to be, you mean?" Brooke corrected him.

"That's what I said."

Starr laughed and said, "This ain't no damn meeting spot."

"Look, auntie. Don't blame me. Q told me to meet him here." Starr huffed, then seconds later Q walked through the door. Starr and Q's eyes met and held. Seconds later, Starr said, "I want to speak to you before you leave."

DeMontre followed Q outside and before he left, he looked back when Starr's back was turned. He made eye contact with Brook and winked. He pretended that he held a phone to his ear and signaled to Brooke, "Call me."

Q returned then followed Starr back into the office. When the door was shut, she said, "So why are you and DeMontre meeting over here every week?"

He laughed and said, "If you don't want me to meet here, I won't meet him here. I just thought this was a good meeting point, nothing more. Nothing less."

"Look, Q, we are not seeing each other."

"We're on break."

"So why are you trying to stay in touch with my family?"

"The young boy wanted to make some extra money and I thought I would help him."

Starr huffed and said, "I know you have the best intentions, but the fact of the matter is, you're a drug dealer. Not just a drug dealer but a drug boss, and this is doing more harm than good. He sees you riding around town in your cars and shit and not working and he's going to think this is what life is about."

"I don't discuss business with him. Are you crazy? He's a kid."

"You don't have to discuss business with him. He's not slow. He knows what you do."

Q frowned then said, "I understand, but it's not like he's an honor roll student. Just the other day he asked me if I wanted some loud. Said he had the best loud in the A."

"I know he ain't innocent, but I don't want you to corrupt him further."

"So I'm corrupt?"

"I didn't mean it like that."

"You have a good day, Starr."

Chapter 21

TETE WAS SURPRISED WHEN SHE SAW THAT ELI WAS calling her repeatedly. She didn't want to answer the phone, but he was so persistent that she finally answered. She'd been watching Power on DVR so she stood and paused the DVR.

"Eli," she said into the phone.

"Hey, babe."

"Cut the 'hey, babe' shit."

"I need to see you."

"About what?"

"I can't say over the phone."

"You know where I live."

"Give me twenty minutes."

TeTe opened the door for Eli. Eli wore a white, V-neck T-shirt and jeans. He was looking very buffed and his skin glowed. She could tell he had been working out and that he was taking very good care of himself. She looked down at the phantom finger and for a brief moment, she felt very sorry for him. But then she thought about all the bullshit he had taken her through with all the different women.

"Thanks for letting me come over," he said.

"What the fuck do you want?"

"Can I sit down?"

She led him into the kitchen. They sat at the bar beside each other. There was an awkward silence then finally she said, "You've been working out."

"I have but I had to get used to working out with a missing finger. It was hard." He laughed but she ignored it.

She didn't want to think about what she had done to his finger and as far as she was concerned, he deserved that.

"Did you miss me?"

"Butterfly does."

"I miss her, too."

TeTe folded her arms and looked away.

"Goddamn, you're looking good and smelling good."

She thought the same about him. His sexy ass was looking good too, especially, with the new physique.

"You have something you want to tell me?"

"It's about Todd."

"What about him?"

"He came to see me at my mama's house a few weeks ago. Him and some niggas from out of Detroit."

TeTe's eyebrows raised. "What did he want?"

"He said you murdered his cousin and he wanted revenge. The Detroit dudes said something about you killing their brother and they were asking all kinds of questions about how security worked over here. They were wanting to know all kinds of shit like if I knew the code to the alarm. Wanting to know if your mom lived in Atlanta? You know weird shit like they were going to try to do something crazy."

She folded her arms. "So it's true. This is the second time, I heard this story."

"I wouldn't lie to you."

"Of course not." She looked down at his missing finger.

A pitcher of lemonade sat on the counter across from the bar. Eli stood and retrieved a glass out of the cabinet. TeTe was in deep thought, and when Eli realized that he hadn't asked if he could have the lemonade he said. "Do you mind?" He pointed toward the pitcher of lemonade.

"When have you known me to care about some petty-ass lemonade?"

He laughed. Same old TeTe. She'll never change. Always hardcore.

"Do you know how to get in touch with these clowns?" she asked.

"No." He filled the glass up with lemonade and crushed ice then sat back at the bar. "I thought you might want to know this. That's the only reason I was blowing up your phone."

"How long had you known this?"

"For a few weeks."

"And you just now tell me this bullshit?"

"I'm sorry. I tried to call you a couple of times and you kept sending me to voicemail."

She knew what he was saying was true. "You should have just texted."

"You're right."

Their eyes met and held for a long time before he downed the lemonade, stood and said, "I gotta go."

"Stay." She put her arms around his waist and said, "I missed you."

"I missed you too." It was hell staying at his mama's house. Being a grown-ass man with no job skills and no money. He spent most of his days at the gym working out.

"Too bad you ain't at your other mama's house."

"Huh?"

"Me." She leaned into him and kissed him. Her breath refreshing. She smelled like vanilla and it was turning him the fuck on. They stood up from the barstools and peeled off their clothes. She hopped up on the kitchen table and he stood back and admired her body.

She thought about Black briefly before deciding that she knew his ass was being unfaithful. Her clit was now throbbing and needed attention. She knew Eli would know exactly how to give it to her. He made his way toward her; his dick looked so succulent to her. Her legs gaped open, waiting on his arrival. Seconds later, he climbed on a chair that was in front of the table. He began nibbling and licking her thighs.

His tongue was making a trail to her VJ and when he was inches away, she grabbed his head and said, "Come on. Dive in. Mama missed you."

He wanted to do exactly that but he wanted to take his time and relish the moment. Enjoy what he didn't appreciate when he had it.

· · ·

Brooke was leaning against the counter and checking her Snapchat when Starr walked up behind her and startled her. Brooke turned and faced her.

Starr said, "I'm sorry. I didn't mean to startle you."

"It's okay."

Starr gave Brooke a once over. She was dressed very nicely in a navy-blue romper and she was carrying a Chanel bag that cost three thousand dollars. Starr knew this because she'd priced the bag herself and she was going to buy it, but at the last minute, she decided not to. But here was her seventeen-year-old employee with the bag that she had wanted.

"I love the romper."

"Thank you. Forever 21."

"And the bag?"

"It was a gift from my father."

Starr knew Brooke's father was an anesthesiologist. He made a great salary but, even for him, this bag was very expensive to buy a kid. His wife maybe, but who was she to tell someone how to spend their money?

"I have a question to ask you."

"Is it about your nephew?"

"Yes. Did you go out with him the other night?"

Brook avoided eye contact, but finally she said, "I did."

Starr huffed and said, "Look, Brooke. I love you and I love my nephew. He's a good kid, but I don't think that he's a good boyfriend for you. I thought you had a boyfriend?"

Brooke was too embarrassed so she turned away.

Starr wrapped her arms around her and said, "Look, I know my nephew is funny and exciting, but right now, he's doing things that he shouldn't be doing. And the last thing I want you to do is get into trouble hanging out with his ass."

Brooke turned and met Starr's gaze and said, "How did you find out?"

"Did you think I wasn't going to find out?"

"Was it Mr. Q?"

"Wait a minute. Did he know about you and him seeing each other?"

"I don't know. But DeMontre came to my house in Mr. Q's Range Rover."

"Oh, really?"

"Yes."

"Where did y'all go?"

"To Atlantic Station. We went to the movies then we went the South DeKalb Mall."

"South DeKalb Mall? Why did y'all go there?"

"Because I had never been. He said he wanted to show me what the 'Hood Mall' looked like." She laughed.

"What did you think?"

"Too ghetto for me, but the people were nice."

"Look, my nephew is a drug dealer. Did you know that?"

"No."

"Yes, him and his twin brother push bags of weed out of his mama's house. I don't want you seeing him again. If you go out with him again, I'm telling your parents. And if that don't work, I'm firing you."

"He just needs a good girl."

"You can't change him. He's the way he is."

"Like you couldn't change Mr. Trey? Like you can't change Mr. Q?"

Starr became angry. "What the hell did you say?"

"I'm sorry."

Starr wanted to slap the fuck out of this little girl. Who was she to tell her what she couldn't do? But the more she thought about it, Brooke was right.

"Look, Brooke, I don't want you to make the same mistakes I made."

"I'm sorry. I shouldn't have said that."

"No, it's true. I did try to change those men and I couldn't.

But you see, there are a few differences. Like I grew up in the hood and I was an adult when I started dating hustlers."

"I know. I'm sorry and I'll tell him that I can't see him no more. I hated hiding that from you, but he told me not to tell you that I was seeing him."

"Cuz he knew that I wouldn't go for that shit. I would not sit there and let him ruin your life."

"He's that bad, huh?"

"Not bad, just a victim of his circumstances. His mother is trifling as hell."

"Your sister, right?"

"What is that supposed to mean?"

"Did you break up with Mr. Q because he hustles?"

There was a long silence. This little girl was just too goddamned nosey for her own good.

"I don't know why I broke up with Q."

"Was there another woman?"

"No. Why do you ask?"

"Oh, nothing."

"Do you know something?"

"Well, the other day when DeMontre picked me up, I saw a scrunchie in the car."

"Oh, really?"

"Yeah."

"Thanks for telling me that."

Starr tried to stay strong, but Brooke saw the hurt in her eyes.

"I didn't want to tell you that."

"It's not your fault, honey."

"One more thing. I lied to you."

"About what?"

"This bag."

"You did. Why?"

"Your nephew bought it for me."

"What? That's a three thousand dollar bag. Where in the fuck did he get money to buy this kind of bag? Peddling bags of weed didn't do it, that's for damn sure."

Brooke shrugged her shoulders.

"I'm going to get to the bottom of this."

•   •   •

Q was taken aback when Starr showed up unannounced. She strolled right in without even saying hello.

"What brings you here?"

"You know what brings me here. First of all, you letting my nephew drive all around town in a hundred thousand dollar car."

"What the hell are you talking about? You already know I let him wash my car."

"And you let him pick up dates in the car."

"What?"

"Brooke said that he picked her and her friend up and took them to Atlantic Station and to the mall in your vehicle."

Q studied Starr's face. He knew she was feisty but he had never seen her this angry. "Look, I didn't know nothing about that." Q thought. "Ok, when was this? Was it Saturday?"

"I think so."

"Ok, it did take him a while to finish the car but he told me that his friend at the detail spot couldn't let him use the equipment because he was busy." Q laughed and said, "So what? He was trying to impress some girls with a car. Everybody has done that. That's part of growing up."

"You think it's funny?"

Q sighed and said, "Relax, baby. The kid is just being a kid."

"Him and his brother are some petty-ass hustlers and the last thing that they need to do is be around somebody that they look up to."

"Yeah, I told you that he asked me if I needed some loud."

"Did you know that he bought Brooke a Chanel bag?"

"No idea and what the hell does that got to do with me?"

"The bag cost three thousand dollars."

"Might have been a knockoff?"

"It's the real thing. I was about to get the bag myself but the price made me put it back."

"Hey, I didn't give him the money. I gave him a couple of hundred dollars."

Q sounded convincing. Starr knew that her nephews were unruly as hell, and she knew that they were headed down a destructive path with or without Q. She turned and walked toward the door.

Q said, "Was there anything else that you wanted?"

She turned and faced him again, her eyes on his chest. She missed him and she wished that she could rest her head on his chest. She wanted him to pull her close and tell her that he missed her too.

"Is there anything else?"

"Not really?"

"So you didn't miss me?"

"You know I did but—"

"But what?"

"But you have someone and she's pretty and she'd educated. She's the total package."

"I don't have anyone."

"So you haven't been out with anyone?"

"I didn't say that." He paused then pulled her near him and gave her forehead a kiss just like she had wanted. She wanted to melt. She wanted to pull him close and rip that shirt off him. She wanted to make love to him, but instead, she pulled away from him.

He made a sad face when she pulled away.

"What's wrong, baby?"

"Well Brooke spotted a scrunchie and a thong in your Range Rover." Starr lied about the thong but he didn't need to know that.

"If there was a thong there, it had to be her thong." Q laughed. "A scrunchie, maybe, but a thong? No way."

"So you haven't slept with her?"

He was silent. He knew there was no easy way to answer this. He knew that the right thing to do was to tell her the truth, but he knew that if he was honest, it would crush her.

"Answer me, Q?"

He didn't answer. He strolled to the other side of the room and instead of using the button for the electric blinds, he pulled them back manually and glanced out into the city.

"You're not going to answer me?"

"Yes, we had sex. I'm not going to lie , but he was lying, he knew she was lying about the thong so he decided to lie too.

"What?"

"Who have you been sleeping with, Ms. Goody Two-Shoes."

"I can't believe you asked me that. What kind of woman do you think I am?"

"Hey, I just asked a question."

"Q...I'll see you later, Q." She bee lined toward the door.

Q wanted to run and jump in front of her and stop her but he decided against that. Instead, he yelled, "You're the one that wanted to take a break! What did you expect me to do?"

"I expected you to do exactly what you did."

"You know what, Starr. You don't know how to be loved. You're not ready for love. That's your problem. Come see me when you're ready to be loved."

"Whatever, Q. Go fuck your little friend with her uppity ass."

Chapter 22

FBI AGENT DANIELS SHOWED UP AT SASHA'S HOME RIGHT around 8 a.m. Daniels removed the hidden surveillance cameras from the smoke detectors and the hidden recording devices from the nightstand. She was relieved the investigation of her father was coming to an end and soon he would be arrested so she could achieve some sort of normalcy in her life. And even though he was a horrible monster of a man that had molested her since she was a little girl, she felt bittersweet about helping the Feds bring him down. As weird and disgusting as it seemed, she did love him.

Daniels embraced her before she jerked away from him. He said, "I know this must have been hard for you, but you did the right thing. In time, you'll feel better."

"You think so?"

"I know so." He tried to embrace her again but she didn't allow it.

"If this is all you need from me?"

"Yes, this is all we need. You got him to admit that he was hiding the money. This is all that we need. We're going to get the grand jury to seek an indictment."

"You think you're going to get it?"

"It's almost certain that we're going to get it."

Sasha smiled then asked, "Are you going to be able to help my friend out?"

"Brooks?"

"Yes."

"I don't know, to be honest. We can try, but more than likely, he's stuck. Sasha, you were a victim and we wanted to help you. And that's all we're concerned about now."

"But you said you would help."

"We'll try. We can ask the AUSA if they would consider giving him a time cut. That's all we can ask for him."

That's not the answer she wanted to hear and it was damn sure not the answer that Black wanted to hear. But it was an answer. She could tell Black, but there was nothing that she could do.

* * *

Craig had injected fat taken from Fy-head's abdomen into her ass about a week ago, and it had been almost ten days since he'd given J-Will the money for the murder. The job had not been completed nor had he heard from anyone. The number that J-Will had given him was going straight to voice mail. Luckily for him, after he had performed the surgery on Fy-head, he'd taken her home so he had her home address.

He decided to pay her a visit. He parked his car on the side of the road and as soon as he got out of the car, a police patrol car drove up. Before he could ask what the problem was, the two officers hopped out of the car, leaving the car in the middle of the road with the lights flashing. Both officers were six feet tall. One was an Asian with a goatee and the other was a black guy with a low haircut. The black officer looked like he spent most of his free time at the gym. His name tag identified him as Simmons and the Asian guy's name tag said Xiong.

Simmons was chewing Bubble Yum. "So what are you doing over here?"

"Going to visit a friend."

"This is a drug infested neighborhood," Xiong said.

"I didn't know that."

"What's your friend's name?"

"Cassandra."

Xiong said, "Can I see your ID?"

"My ID? For what? I haven't done anything!"

Xiong looked at him and said, "You're going to lower your voice or else."

"Or else what?"

Simmons was standing there with a stupid-ass grin on his face, cracking his knuckles and blowing bubbles but didn't say a word. Craig glanced at the size of his ape-sized hands. Craig knew he was no match for the two officers.

Craig made eye contact with Xiong and said, "Why do you want to see my ID?"

Xiong stepped forward and when he and Craig were inches apart, he said, "Because...you... don't... belong ... here."

Simmons blew a huge bubble and when it popped, it stuck to his face. He removed it from his mustache with his index finger and said, "We said show us your ID and you can go on your way. If not, we're going to want to search your car."

Craig laughed at the two asshole cops and said, "For what reason? There is absolutely no probable cause."

"Oh yeah?" Xiong inched toward Craig's car, kneeled down and picked up a small Ziploc baggie with cocaine residue. He then made his way back over to Craig and glanced at the black officer. "Probable cause."

"Not mine."

"Who's going to believe you? White man in a black neighborhood. What the hell are you doing here?"

Craig hadn't come to buy drugs, but he wasn't certain that his car was clean. He couldn't remember if he had drug paraphernalia in the car or not. He removed the license and handed it to the asshole cop who examined the license and handed it back to him

"See how simple that was?" the cop said.

"So where are you going?"

"What do you mean?"

"Which house is your friend's?"

Craig pointed to the green house. A man and a woman were on the porch smoking a cigarette and as soon as they noticed Craig pointing, they disappeared inside.

Simmons started laughing and said, "He's going to the Ho house."

"What?"

Simmons popped his Bubble Yum and said, "Now, come on, bro. Don't act like you don't know that's a Ho house."

"A whore house?"

"You say whore house, I say Ho house. You say tomato I say to-mah-to."

"Look, I don't know anything about that."

"Sure you don't. Just let me tell you, if the vice raid that house, your ass is going to jail."

The Asian cop turned to his partner and said, "Come on, let's go. The car is in the middle of the street."

Seconds later, they jumped in the patrol car and screeched off with the lights still flashing.

Craig got out of his car and headed for the house. When he reached the front door he rang the doorbell.

A man answered the door. A different man than the one that had been smoking a cigarette earlier.

The black man was about fifty, with graying hair. He was thin and had tired eyes. "How can I help you?" he asked.

"I'm looking for Cassandra." Craig said.

"What you want with Cassandra? Are you the police?"

"Hell, no!"

Seconds later, a fat ugly tranny with a face full of Mary Kay makeup and a blond wig appeared wearing a nightgown. An unlit Newport dangled from her mouth.

"I saw his ass talking to the police. He's fucking Po-Po. Me and Bobby was out here smoking a cigarette and I saw his ass right there in the middle of the road talking to them. He's the fucking Po-Po, man."

Craig didn't know what Po-Po meant but judging by the context of the sentence, he could only assume that Po-Po meant police, which probably was not good in this neighborhood.

"What do you want?"

"I'm just looking for Cassandra."

"Don't no Cassandra live here."

Craig knew they didn't believe him and why should they believe him. He didn't fit in over here. He was the white guy standing in the middle of the road that had just pointed out their house to the police.

The tranny lit her Newport and said, "You need to get the hell away from here and get away from here fast."

"I'm not a cop."

The man named Bobby came out—the one that had been on the porch smoking earlier. Bobby was a skinny motherfucker with a huge nose and flaring nostrils that you could see into. He had the words Evil and Good tatted across his knuckles. Though he was skinny, he definitely didn't look like the kind of motherfucker you wanted to mess with.

Bobby said, "The man asked for Cassandra; he must know her. White boy, how you know Cassandra? You been tricking on her?"

"Oh no, no. Nothing like that."

"Cassandra is HIV positive. Just in case you get the notion to do something like that."

Craig said, "Can you tell me where she is?"

"No, she don't live here no more. I was her boyfriend."

"What do you mean was?"

"We broke up."

"Why?"

"That's none of your business."

"She's HIV?"

"That's none of your business."

"Y'all motherfuckers have run your goddamned mouths too much as it is. I told you this man is the Po-Po," the tranny proclaimed.

"Can you tell me where she is?"

"I don't know."

"If you knew, would you tell me?"

"Hell, no."

This conversation was pointless as far as Craig was

concerned. He said, "I'm going to leave now."

He turned and started to walk away. He was halfway down the steps of the porch when the man named Bobby approached and put a knife to his back. "Not before you leave something."

"Like what?"

"Your wallet."

Craig removed his wallet. "I only have sixty dollars."

"Give me the goddamned money and shut the fuck up if you want to make it out of here alive."

Craig complied. He was halfway to his car when he wondered whether they still thought he was the Po-Po.

Chapter 23

THE MAYOR STAGGERED INTO SASHA'S CONDO AND SHE was surprised that he was still on the street. She had expected them to have picked him up by now. She didn't know how the Feds worked, but she had given them the evidence. She had expected someone from the family to call her and tell her that her daddy had been arrested, but instead, he was right here in her place.

His necktie was loose and his eyes were glassy. She could only assume that he had been drinking. She knew that look.

They stared at each other for a long time before he said, "You got something to drink in here?"

"There is a bottle of Skyy in the cabinet."

"What's that?"

"Vodka."

He stumbled his ass over to the counter and snatched a shot glass from the counter. He poured himself a shot of Skyy and downed it with one swift drink. "You know all I ever did for you was—" He stopped then he looked under the lampshade and scanned the area.

"What are you looking for?"

"Bugs and cameras. You know some people like to play

around with bugs, wires and secret cameras." He grinned.

"What are you talking about?

"Oh, you know what I'm talking about. You know damn well what I'm talking about."

She sat on the sofa and watched him closely as he almost knocked over the coffee table.

"Watch where you're going!"

"You don't tell me what the fuck to do. I tell you what to do." He plopped down on the sofa beside her and stared at her with those glassy eyes and said, "Why did you do it to me?"

"Do what?"

"Don't play dumb, bitch."

She tried to ease away but he gripped her wrist and wouldn't let go of it. It was like he had a vice grip on her wrist. She struggled with him but couldn't break free. She used her other hand to try to pry his fingers off her wrist but she couldn't.

"Didn't I give you everything that you ever wanted?"

"You ruined my life is what you did."

"I ruined your life?" He laughed. "You're the one that wants me to spend my life in a living hell!"

"And you made my life a living hell. How do you think I felt? I'm a thirty-year-old woman that can't have a relationship. Never been in love. Addicted to all sorts of weirdo sex because I have been molested and basically controlled since I was old enough to remember. Let go of my wrist." She tried to shake free from his grip again but couldn't.

"You set me up, bitch, and you didn't think that I was going to find out? What the fuck? Did you think I was stupid?"

"I have no idea what you're talking about."

"Oh, you know exactly what I'm talking about." She kicked him hard on his shin but he still held on to her. Then he pushed her to the floor and pinned her down with both hands. She fought hard with knees and kicks. He ripped her shirt off, exposing her chest.

He placed his vodka smelling mouth on her lips and said, "Give me a kiss."

She resisted and turning her head. Every time he did this, she felt disgusted, and this time, she felt even more disgusted. She spat in his face and he backhanded the fuck out of her. Blood sputtered from her nose down into her mouth like a faucet. He ripped her skirt off and now she was naked except for a pair of electric-blue lace panties.

"No good ho is what you are."

He ripped her panties off and she was naked. She kept struggling, and finally, she broke free and he chased her into the corner. He raised his hands to slap the fuck out of her but she flinched and he grabbed her by the throat and began to strangle her. Then he leaned forward and he met her mouth again. This time, despite the strong vodka stench, she didn't resist. She kissed him passionately like she would do to any of her past lovers. There was a look in her eye that he'd seen so many times before. He loosened his tie and she helped him unbutton his shirt. The pants came off and moments later, the boxers. He stood there butt naked, except for a pair of black church socks. His tiny uncircumcised penis pointing at her.

Nothing about this man made any sense to her. He knew that she had flipped on him to the Feds, but he still wanted to fuck her.

He leaned into her and kissed her. He picked her up and fell with her on the sofa. He was on top of her and they made eye contact. He jugged his fingers into her tight pussy. He was fingering her, trying to get her wet. She wanted to vomit every time he touched her down there.

A look of disappointment came over his face. She had gotten a waxing earlier, hoping that she could convince Black to come over and fuck the shit out her. But her Daddy didn't like it bald. He was old school and he hated it bald, but it was ironic because when he first started touching her she was bald as a baby's head.

She closed her eyes in an attempt to block out what was happening to her. He was rubbing his dick on her thigh, and then seconds later, he was inside her. She felt him thrust.

He said, "Open your eyes."

He always wanted her to open her eyes and this is what she hated most. She hated looking at him. She had his nose and his mouth and almost none of her mother's features. How can a man that gave her so much of himself, take so much away from her?

She opened her eyes and made eye contact with him. His eyes were pink from the liquor and there was dried-up saliva on the side of his mouth. He thrusted and thrusted until she watched him go into convulsions as he came inside of her.

Once he finished, he got up, his dick swinging wildly, as he eased back into the kitchen. He got the bottle of vodka and brought it into the living room. He sat on the sofa, still butt naked except for those stupid-ass church socks pulled all the way up to his knees.

He said, "I guess it's over for me. I'm going to prison for a very long time."

And he downed two more shots of liquor.

She stood and slid back into her panties. He was staring at her body in admiration and when she noticed, she thought to herself, God don't let him go for round two.

He stood and poured himself another shot. Just as he sat down, the glass slipped from his hand and shattered on the floor.

"Motherfucker," he exclaimed and he dropped to his knees to pick up the tiny glass bits that covered the floor.

Sasha made her way over to the floor. Her instincts told her to get a broom to clean up the mess. Instead, she picked up the Skyy bottle from the coffee table and she tried her best to crack his motherfucking cranium. The bottle shattered and knocked his ass out instantly. He was lying in a pool of blood. She checked his pulse. He was still breathing.

She walked over to where his pants were and dug inside his pants pockets. She was going to take his keys with her but she was shocked to find a 9mm gun with a silencer on it. He had come to take her life. It was time to get missing. She was sure there were people who wanted her dead.

Chapter 24

WHEN Q FIRED HIS ENGINE UP, FUTURE'S DIRTY SPRITE 2
blared through the speakers. He lowered the volume in a
hurry and put it on something milder. Every time he got
in his car after DeMontre had driven it, he knew what to
expect—trap music to be blasting.

There was supposed to be thirty-nine hundred dollars
under the armrest. He had put it aside for some tires that
he was going to buy, but when he'd gotten to the rim shop,
the guy told him that the rims didn't hadn't come in. When
he offered to pay, the man told him to just hold on to his
money. He remembered putting the cash under the armrest
and now it was gone. He called DeMontre.

"Hey, Uncle Q."

"Did you see some money under the armrest?'

"No, all I saw was some mail. Why? Is there money missing?"

"I don't know yet."

"How much are you looking for?"

"Close to four thousand dollars."

"Oh hell, naw. I ain't seen money like that Uncle Q."

"I was just asking, bruh. I didn't accuse you of anything."

"Okay as long as you know I ain't do it."

"Who washed the car?" Q said. He opened the glove compartment and there was no sign of the money in there either.

"I washed the car. Why do you ask?"

"I was thinking that maybe you took the car to a car wash and maybe someone from the car wash took the money."

"No, I washed it myself."

"Okay, I'll keep looking for it and if I find it, I will call you."

When Q hung up the phone, he realized that DeMontre had stolen his money. This would explain why he had been able to buy Brooke that handbag. He called Starr but her phone was going to voicemail.

•   •   •

Under the moonlight, Starr and Terrell sipped wine on his patio.

Starr said to Terrell, "I got to get home. My phone is dead."

"Not now." He smiled.

"I can't go home?" She laughed playfully as she admired him.

"I have a charger," he said.

"You're going to get me in trouble."

He stood and poured her another Sangria. "Give me that phone." He examined the phone and passed it back to her. "I thought you had an iPhone?"

"You notice everything."

"I notice everything about you."

"I did, but I got the Samsung Galaxy Edge the other day."

"You like it?"

"The camera is amazing, but you know how it is when you get used to something."

"I know what you mean."

"So, you don't have a charger for the Samsung Galaxy?"

"I ain't say all that."

He disappeared into the house, and she watched his sexy-ass walk. Seconds later, he returned with the charger.

"How do these things work?" she asked.

"Just set your phone on the charger."

She sat her phone on the charger.

He took his seat across from her and said, "I'm so glad you could make it tonight. Actually, when I called you and suggested this to you, I didn't think you would come."

She smiled politely. She didn't think she would come either, but when Q just straight up admitted that he had slept with this new chick, she didn't see any reason to sit in the house and sulk. She had to be a big girl and get out of the house or else she was going to drive herself crazy thinking about what had happened between Q and this Chanel girl.

"You know, that was a lame excuse for having to go home, right?"

"What?" She looked surprised.

"Your phone was dead."

"How was that lame? You know I have a son. What if his grandma tries to call me?"

"Oh, I forgot about your little boy. How is he doing anyway?"

"Growing too big for his clothes every day."

"Oh yeah? What size shoe does he wear?"

"A six in adults."

"Okay, I got some Nike shoes and gear he can have. Nike still sends me stuff."

"He would love that. Though I just got him the Curry 1's."

"Hey, you can never have enough shoes."

"Especially how he's growing."

She finished her glass of wine and he poured another one. "Are you trying to get me drunk?" she asked.

"Maybe, but I'm going to get drunk with you."

She sat her glass down and before she could respond, he shoved his tongue down her throat. She didn't want to resist. He wanted her and she wanted him. Moments later, they had both peeled out of their clothes, He was butt naked and she stood on the patio wearing only a yellow G-string.

When he laid eyes on her body, he said, "I've never seen nothing like that in my life."

Her Chanel No. 5 was intoxicating and he absolutely loved how everything about her was so feminine.

She smiled, revealing dimples that rarely came out unless she was very happy or excited, or both. She glanced down at his tool that was hung right above his knee.

"I want you," he said. "I've always wanted you since the first day I saw you. Your ambition turns me on. You're the kind of woman that I can spend the rest of my life with."

She was smiling and she ran her hands across his deeply etched abs. She could feel the moistness between her legs. He had admitted that he wanted her and as much as she hated to admit it, she had wanted him too.

She took his manhood in her hand and stroked it. He broke free from her and reached for a blue blanket that was lying on one of the patio chairs. With the blanket in his hand, he covered the table with the blanket and laid her across the table. Her legs were open and he looked down at her. She smiled at him. She could tell that this sexy motherfucker really did want her.

For a second, she felt guilty as she thought about Q. Then she thought about how he had fucked that girl so fast. Though she had told him that she wanted to take a break, he shouldn't have gone through with it. This is why she is here with Terrell, she justified.

"I want to please you. I'm here to do anything that you want me to do."

He kissed her thighs and his goatee tickled her. She could tell he was a slow careful but very skilled love maker. He continued to peck her thighs and she clawed his back with her nails. He was gentle with her and she liked that but she could tell that he would be too gentle and take too long as thoughts of Q entered her mind. Finally, she pulled him up to her and said, "Just fuck me and treat me bad."

He said, "Huh?"

"Just fuck me!" She reached for his tool and it was stiff and pulsating. She slid it inside her lovehole and with her nails clenching his back, she told him to go deep inside her.

Terrell was frustrated. He'd wanted to make love to her, but she didn't want that from him. Though he had her body right now, Q still had her heart and mind, and she couldn't help but feel guilty for fucking Terrell.

He turned her over and fucked her doggy-style. Spanking her ass as she let out passionate screams and ordered him to fuck her harder.

The neighbor's porch lit up, but that didn't stop them. He was stroking her until they both came. When she stood up, he was still admiring her body, but he felt used at the same time. There was no passion there. There was plenty of chemistry, but he could tell that she didn't want him in the capacity that he had wanted her.

He put his pants on and said, "How was it?"

"It was amazing."

"You're still in love with him, ain't you?"

There was a brief silence then she said, "Yeah."

"I know."

She gathered her clothes that were still lying on the floor and said, "Where is your shower?"

"You know where it is. You decorated the house, remember?"

She giggled and said, "I did, didn't I?"

She was about to take off in the direction of the bathroom when he said, "Why him?"

"Huh?"

"What does he have that I don't have? What is it? I have money. I'm single. I don't have a bunch of baby mamas. I'm tall. I'm good looking."

Starr stopped in her tracks thinking, what the fuck? Why is this nigga getting all emotional? She sat back on the patio table and said, "Nothing is wrong with you. It's not about you."

"Just answer the question, Starr. Why can't you give me a shot? I mean if it don't work out, at least we will know that we gave it a try."

"You're right."

"Why him?"

"I think I told you. He came along at the right time right after my fiancé was murdered. He was there for me."

"But he's not there for you now; otherwise, you wouldn't be here."

"You're right. Things are a little rocky right now. I will admit that."

"So there's a chance for me and you?"

"There's always a chance for anything."

She hopped off the table, took possession of her phone from the charger and entered his home through the patio door. Her clothes were in her hands. He followed in bare feet, walking over the tile floors.

She took a fifteen minute shower and when she was dressed, he hugged her and walked her to her car. The clock on her dash said it was 1:45 a.m. She powered on her phone, saw that she had a message from Q and dialed his phone number. It went straight to voicemail. He was with that bitch. She could feel it. A tear trickled down her cheek.

Chapter 25

SASHA HAD CALLED BLACK AT TWO IN THE MORNING AND said it was urgent that she see him. She had told him, matter-of-factly, not to come to the condo. Instead, she told him to meet her at the Marriott in Lawrenceville. She said it was urgent and that she needed to see him right away. It was three in the morning before Black made his way to room two twenty-eight. She opened the door and ushered him in right away. She peeked through the blind and was nervous as hell, which was making Black nervous.

Finally he said, "Will you tell me what the fuck is going on?"

"So much!" She paced the floor.

Black's eyes were red from some Trainwreck that he'd smoked earlier, and he was hungry as hell. There was a box holding a cheese pizza from Papa John's on the edge of the bed, so he grabbed a slice.

Sasha was still pacing and she said, "There is some Coke that came free with the pizza. It's in the fridge. You can have it if you want."

Black made his way over to the fridge and grabbed a can of Coke, folded the pizza in half and swallowed it whole. Then he washed it down with the Coke and said, "Will you please tell me what the fuck is going on?"

"Look, I told you about my dad. Told you I was going to give him up."

"Yeah, you told me and you also said you would ask for a time cut for my boy."

"I did, but I don't think they're going to do it."

Black grabbed another slice of pizza then took a seat. "Now, tell me what happened."

"He found out."

"Who found out?"

"My dad found out that I went to the FBI."

"Oh yeah? How did he find out?"

"I don't know."

Black ate the pizza with one bite, finished the Coke and then let out a loud burp.

She was still pacing and said again, "I know he found out though."

"How do you know he found out?"

"He came over and he was saying all this shit about how I wasn't loyal to him and he was checking for bugs and cameras and shit. Then he just straight up said to me that I didn't think that he was going to find out. But he said he has a way of knowing everything. Then he raped me and he was going to try to kill me."

"No way!"

She presented him with the gun with the silencer.

Black reached for it before deciding not to put his fingerprints on it.

"I'm not touching it." He paused. "How did you get it?"

"I knocked him unconscious with a vodka bottle."

"What?"

"Yeah, I took the bottle and knocked his ass unconscious and when I checked his pockets, this is what I found."

"Damn, he was really going to take you out."

"You think? I know he's still going to get me, I can just feel it. I need you to be here with me."

"I can't be here with you, I got shit to do. Shit to take care of."

She looked disappointed and she said, "Of course, you can't stay with me. You never can. I'm just a piece of ass to you."

"That ain't true."

"Prove it to me."

There was a brief silence and then he said, "I can't stay with you."

"Who's going to protect me, Black? If you don't protect me, who will?"

"You have the gun. Do you know how to shoot?"

She aimed the gun at him and said, "I don't know. Let's find out."

Her hands trembled and Black was trying to read this bitch. Was she for real?

"Put the gun down, Sasha. Put the fucking gun down. It's going to be alright."

Tears rolled down her face and she said, 'How the fuck do you know it's going to be alright?"

"It always is. It just always is."

"What the fuck? It always is? What kind of answer is that?"

"Look, Sasha, nobody is going to kill you." He lowered his voice and he was looking at the silencer on the end of the gun and he thought about his family. Especially his children. This is how Trey went out. A crazy bitch. He didn't want to go out like that.

"Look, if you can give me two days, I'll be back. I'll be back and I'll take care of you."

"Remember the men that kidnapped you? Those motherfuckers, Black. They're after me. Trained killers."

Black remembered the white boys that had thrown him into the van. They were some real motherfuckers, that was for sure. He looked Sasha in the eyes and said, "If God is for us, who can be against us?"

"Huh?"

"If God is for us, we're going to be okay, even against assassins."

She lowered the gun and Black embraced her. She cried on his shoulder and he said, "Just remember, if God is for us...."

"I'm scared. I'm scared that they are going to find us."

"If God is for us," he whispered.

•   •   •

Starr was in her office invoicing customers when Brooke came running to the back to tell her that Q was out front.

"Send him back." Starr said.

Seconds later, Q walked back to the office and Starr looked up, designer glasses draping her face.

He said, "I didn't know you wore glasses."

"Just to read."

"You look cute in them."

She smiled and said, "So, are you here to meet my nephew again?"

"Actually not at all. I'm here to tell you that I think your nephew took some money that don't belong to him. I tried calling you last night to tell you, but you didn't answer the phone. You must have been busy."

"I returned the call."

"Yeah, at like two in the morning. Was he gone then?"

"Excuse me?"

"Did you call after he left? Come on, Starr. You ain't got to lie to me. I just got a feeling that you have been seeing that basketball player. All girls want one."

"Whatever, Q. I ain't got time for your games."

He sighed and said, "I didn't come for that anyway. I came to let you know your nephew is a thief. He denied taking it, but I know he did."

"What makes you so sure?"

"Because I'm also missing two kilos."

"What?"

"He was at the crib the other day hanging out on the patio with some girl."

"Brooke?"

"No, another girl."

"I had to run to the mall and I told him to lock up when he was gone. I had nine kilos in my closet because one of my customers from Tennessee was coming to get it. When I counted today, there were only seven. He stole my shit."

"So what do you want me to do about it?"

"Just let him know, I know he got it. I'm not going to do nothing to him because I have too much respect for your family and I love you too much. But I know he's got it."

"No, this is fucked up." Starr paced. "I hate thieves. I'll get to the bottom of this shit for you."

"There is nothing to get to the bottom of. He has it. I mean in the long run, it's going to hurt him more than it's going to hurt me. He'll go out and make his li'l bit of money then fuck it all up on electronics and bitches and then he'll be broke again."

"Look, I'll call you tomorrow to let you know what I found out."

"Don't worry about. When I say it's nothing, I really mean it's nothing."

"It must be something or else you wouldn't be here."

"I just came by to tell you that he must have gotten the money from me. He's stole it."

•   •   •

After three days of calling Fy-Head, Craig called Miss America to his hotel room. He'd said he had some money to spend. But after the last time when she had difficulty getting her money from him, she had told him to call TeTe and book her through the agency. But he didn't have five thousand to pay for that so he told TeTe that he wanted a fifteen-minute conversation with Miss America. For that, TeTe charged one thousand dollars and she sent Eli with Miss America to collect the money. After Craig passed Eli the money, Eli stood outside the hotel room waiting for Craig's fifteen minutes to be up.

When the door was closed, Craig said, "Where the hell is your friend?"

"Who?"

"Cassandra."

"I don't know, I haven't heard from her in days."

Craig began to pace and run his fingers through his hair at the same time. He looked nervous as hell and he was making her nervous.

"What's wrong, honey? You look worried."

"You remember the other day when you were over here and I asked about the job I needed?"

Miss America was in deep thought. "I don't remember."

"The job concerning my wife."

"Yeah."

"I met up with Cassandra and some guy named J-Will. Does that ring a bell?"

"No."

Craig stopped pacing and made eye contact and said, "You mean to tell me you've never heard of this person?"

"Never. I don't run in the same crowd as her. Sure we're both trannies but that don't mean we're both in the same class."

"What the hell does that mean?"

"It means we're not besties, bitch." She rolled her eyes thinking this stupid-ass cracker was making her sick.

"Look. I'm sorry. I'm sorry for bringing this to you. You didn't have anything to do with it but it's just I had given them the money for the job and the next day, Cassandra came over and I gave her fat injections in her ass. She said the job was going to be done. The job is not done and I'm out fifteen thousand dollars."

"Fifteen grand?"

"Yeah."

"What the fuck?"

"Can you call her for me?" Craig looked sad and she felt sorry for him. She removed her phone from her clutch and dialed Fy-Head's number but the phone when straight to voicemail.

"I can go to her house and ask some of our mutual friends if they know where she is. That's all I can do."

Craig extended his hand and they shook hands. "Thanks so much for your help."

She smiled and went outside where Eli was waiting on her. She dialed her phone and when Fy-head picked up, she said, "Bitch, you owe me one." And they both laughed their asses off.

•   •   •

Black had received three calls back to back from Sasha but he had been busy and didn't have time to talk. He had spent some time with his children and he had vowed that he would get back with her later. When he checked his voice mail the last time, she had said that she was going to take a nap. She asked him to come over and spend the night like he had promised. It was 9:45 p.m. when he headed to her hotel room and it was about 10:15 p.m. when he got there. When he opened the door, she was gone, but he was certain he had seen her car out front. He called her name out, but didn't get a response. None at all.

The bathroom door was open and the water was running. As soon as he entered the bathroom, he found her butt naked, hanging, her neck encased with an extension cord, her eyes open, her mouth ajar, her face now a dark purplish color. Black quivered before placing his fingers over her pulse. None.

Then he yelled, "Oh no! No! No! No! You didn't go out like that!"

He didn't know whether to take her body down or leave it up. He'd never experienced anything like this. He ran back out into the bedroom and there was a note on the table.

Dear Black,

I imagine, when you find this note, it will have been too late as with most things in my life. But I want you to know that I loved you and I guess if I had to compare it to anything, I guess it would be in the capacity that you loved Lani. But anyway, I called you and you weren't there for me. The story of my life. But anyway with me out the way, the business is one hundred percent yours and your sister's. I guess that's one good thing. But anyway, just wanted to let you know I love you and if God is for us, right?????

Sasha.

• • •

KINGPIN WIFEYS II,
Part 6: The Wages of Sin

Chapter 1

LAW ENFORCEMENT SWARMED THE HOTEL PARKING LOT.
Patrolmen, homicide detectives and even members of the
F.B.I. were investigating the suicide of Sasha Anderson.

The hotel room was roped off with yellow Do Not Enter tape
and Black had just witnessed Sasha's body being zipped
into a body bag.

A homicide detective named Green read and studied the
suicide note before zip-locking it in with the rest of the
evidence. Green was a middle-aged black man with graying
hair and a thick mustache. He was a short man with large
feet that looked awkward for his stature.

Black recognized Green from when he had been brought
downtown for questioning on the triple homicide. Green
was investigating another murder and he was in the
interrogation room beside the room Black had been in. He
didn't seem to remember Black.

Green called Black outside and began to ask the same
questions repeatedly. "What is your name? How do you
know Sasha? Were you her boyfriend? How long did the two
of you know each other? Were y'all romantically involved?
Did she have any reason to kill herself? How did you find

her? What time did you find her? Did you call the police as soon as you found her? Have you ever been charged with a crime?"

He didn't want to answer that last question but he knew that it was just a matter of time before they found out that he had been charged with crimes.

One of the detectives came back after running his name thought the NCIC database and said, "Mr. Massey, you have quite a lengthy arrest record."

"I do, but I ain't killed her. I loved her."

The man eyed Black skeptically.

After another hour of interrogation, the police hauled him down to the station for further debriefing. The media had shown up but Black refused to answer any questions. It was two a.m. when he was finally released.

•   •   •

The warm air hummed through the vent of TeTe's Jaguar. TeTe's head was wrapped in a navy blue silk scarf and she wore matching silk pajamas and house slippers. She'd been in bed when she got the call from Black. She was parked in an empty parking lot across from the jail. He climbed into her car and they rode for about two minutes in silence before she said, "So do you want to tell me what all of this is about?"

"A friend of mine...committed suicide."

"Wonder what made him do that? Things must have been really bad, huh?"

"What made her do that?"

"It was a bitch?"

TeTe whipped into a B.P. gas station and parked.

Black said, "Can you bring me a Gatorade?"

"I ain't no Gatorade-fetcher. Get your own Gatorade. I ain't getting out of the car."

"What the hell is your problem? How are you going to flip on me that fast?"

She turned the ignition off. "You wanna tell me how you know this bitch?"

"Huh? What?" Black turned the heat off in the car because he was roasting.

"Your little crazy friend that killed herself."

"I know you're not serious."

He made eye contact with TeTe. She crossed her arms. Her bottom lip poked out. "How did you meet her?"

There was a long silence. TeTe crossed her arms and said, "Just as I thought. You were fucking her."

Black sighed and said, "Look, I don't want to argue. I ain't in the mood for arguing and I damn sure don't feel like answering a whole lot of questions."

She fired up the ignition and said, "So, where do you want me to take you? I can take you to your baby mama's house if you want me to."

Black looked at her with pleading eyes and said, "I need to crash at your spot tonight."

"Where is your car?"

Black was trying to think of a lie. A story that made sense to her about why his car was still at the hotel. It was time to be honest. "Turn the car off."

After she deaded the ignition, Black spent the next ten minutes informing her about his history with Sasha. He admitted that he was once her lover and that they were business partners and that she was the mayor of Atlanta's daughter. He told her how she had been hiding out in a hotel. How she had been molested and how the mayor was accepting bribes. He told her about Sasha deciding to work as a CI for the F.B.I.

"So, basically, you made it your job to try to rescue this emotionally damaged ho'?"

"If that's what you want to call it."

"That's what I wanna call it. And not only was she emotionally damaged, she was a snitch."

"I know you don't understand."

"So when is the last time you fucked her, Black?"

"I don't know."

Her eyes narrowed. "Were you fucking her since you've been fucking me?"

"I don't know."

"You know what? Get the fuck out."

"Where am I gonna go?"

"Leave."

"Listen to me."

"I don't want to hear this shit, Black!" She pressed down on the horn nonstop and several patrons of the store were looking in their direction.

"Get the fuck out, Black, or I'm going to scream. I'll scream rape and your black ass will go back to jail!"

He yanked her arm and she tried unsuccessfully to break free.

"Look, I don't have a car or a cell phone and it's three in the morning." His phone was in the trunk of the car at the hotel. Before he called the police, he had stashed it in the trunk and used the room phone to dial 911 because he knew there were going to be lots of questions about the suicide and he was right.

TeTe swung her fist and hit Black with a flurry of punches in his chest and shoulder. "I hate your ass so much right now. I knew I should have followed my gut and my gut was telling me that you ain't shit."

Black grabbed her hands and held her and she said, "You black motherfucker."

TeTe pressed down on the horn again. A wanna-be-hero white man, skinny with spectacles and a beard approached the car.

"Is everything okay, ma'am?"

Black said, "Everything is fine."

The hero had his cell phone in his hand and was about to dial 911. "I wanna hear her say it or I'm calling the police."

TeTe was now calm. She said, "I'm fine, sir. Thanks for your concern."

"I'm sorry, babe. I swear I'm sorry."

"Sorry for what? You told me that you didn't do anything with her while you were with me."

"I don't know, babe, and that's the truth. I've been in and out of jails and hospitals. One of my best friends got murdered. Days are running in to each other."

His eyes were serious and she wanted to believe him and though she didn't want to admit it, her heart was already with him. She loved him. She had fucked Eli a few days ago, but Eli was not the kind of man that Black was. Black was the kind of man that she was used to. She had fallen for him and she hated herself for that.

"I need you and I don't have anyone I can depend on."

He leaned toward her and she blinked as they locked lips. He slid his hand into her bra and cupped her breast. Her nipple was now alive and her mind wanted to tell him to get the fuck out the car but she was aroused.

He rested his head on her shoulder. His beard stubble brushed against her face. He nibbled her earlobe as he whispered, "I love you, TeTe."

She found herself ignoring the voices in her head that told her he was full of shit and said, "I love you, baby! I love you so much and I'll help in any way I can." She buttoned up her shirt and said, "Let's wait until we get home. We can't do it here." She fired up the Jaguar and they darted out of the parking lot.

●　　●　　●

Meeka came to the door wearing a robe and sipping on a forty ounce of Colt 45. She was surprised to look through the peephole and see her sister standing in front of the door. She opened the door but blocked Starr from entering.

"Meeka, can I come in?" Starr asked.

Meeka took a swig from her forty and said, "I'm surprised that you took time away from your charmed life to come to the hood."

"I'm sorry things went wrong the last time that I saw you."

Starr hadn't spoken to her sister since the day that Meeka had embarrassed her in front of Q.

"Why are you here?"

"DeMontre."

"What about DeMontre?"

"Have you seen him?"

"I told him and DeVante to get the fuck out of my house. I know you know that."

"They didn't tell me. I need to tell you something really important."

Meeka stepped aside and led Starr into the kitchen. Music blared through a Bluetooth speaker that was connected to her phone.

Starr plopped down in a chair at the kitchen table and Meeka said, "I would offer you something to drink but I know you don't drink malt liquor."

"Meeka, would you cut the bullshit out. You know that I don't think I'm better than you. I love you, girl."

"You don't act like it." Tears formed in Meeka's eyes. Starr came to the other side of the table and tried to embrace her.

"What's wrong?"

Meeka looked at her with icy eyes and said, "Don't try to hug me. Like you're ashamed of me or something."

"I'm sorry if you feel that way. I didn't know you felt like that."

"You hurt my feelings, Starr."

"Well, you were embarrassing me. Saying that Q was my sugar daddy and all of that. How do you think that made me feel?"

"You know I was only joking. You know how I am."

Starr embraced Meeka and this time she didn't resist.

"I'm okay." Meeka dried her eyes and said, "This is embarrassing. I'm in here acting like a big-ass baby. Let me get myself together."

"You're my big sister and I love you."

Meeka twisted the top on the forty and stashed it back in the fridge then returned to her seat. She said, "So, you were saying something about my son?"

"He took some drugs from Q."

"How much?"

"A lot."

"How much is a lot?"

"A few ki's."

"What?"

"Yeah."

"I'm going to kill that motherfucker when I see him." Meeka made her way back over to the fridge and seized the forty again. "I'm going to need this."

"Q had been letting him do some odd jobs for some money."

"Washing the car, right?"

"Right."

"He told me about that. As a matter of fact, he'd brought Q's car over here one day last week. He had a little girl with him. Pretty little brown girl, talked and acted white, said she worked for you."

"Brooke."

"How do you know he took it?"

"He bought Brooke a Chanel bag."

Meeka took a swig on the beer and said, "He bought that little heifer a Chanel bag and I need new furniture? He could have furnished the whole house for what he paid for that bag."

Starr couldn't believe that Meeka was concerned about what DeMontre had bought Brooke instead of what he had took from Q.

"Do you know where he is?"

"I already told you that I haven't seen him or DeVante in a few days."

"Call them."

"Why don't you get Brooke to call him?"

"Because you're his mother."

Meeka stood took another swig of her beer and said, "I ain't take shit from you or Q."

Starr said, "You're right, but he's going to take something from the wrong motherfucker one day and you're going to end up burying your damn son. Is that what you want?"

"Are you threatening me?" Meeka set the bottle down on the table and said, "Because, bitch, if you want to fight, we can fight right now."

"I didn't come here for all of that." Starr made her way to the door. She was about to let herself out when Meeka said, "Look, Starr, I'm sorry and if DeMontre took something from Q, that's wrong. I'll call him." She removed her cell phone from her pocket and dialed the number, but the phone went straight to voicemail.

"He's not answering, but when he calls back, I'll find out where the fuck he is. You can believe that shit."

"Thanks."

•   •   •

Jada didn't want to answer the private number but at the last moment she did.

"Hey."

She recognized the voice right away. It was Black.

"Can I talk to you?" Black asked.

"About?"

"Look, I got a lot of shit going on and I needed someone to listen. A friend of mine killed herself."

"No!"

"Yeah."

"I'll text you my address."

"I'll be there in fifteen minutes."

An hour later Black showed up at Jada's new place. They sat in the den and drank Heinekens.

"You've been crying?"

"I haven't." He took a swallow from his beer.

"Your eyes are red."

"I haven't slept all night."

"What?"

"Yeah, I found her dead. She hung herself in the shower."

"You found who?"

"My friend, Sasha."

Jada sipped her beer then narrowed her eyes. "What was so bad?"

Black made eye contact with Jada. There was so much that he could have told Jada but instead he said, "It's complicated."

"Did she want to be with you, Black?"

"No. Not at all." Black laughed at that idea and said, "I can assure you, I'm not the bad guy in this situation. But the police questioned me all night. They sure as hell thought I had something to do with it."

"How close were you?"

"Really close."

"I never heard you mention her before."

"We were business partners."

"Were y'all lovers?"

Black avoided her gaze. "What makes you ask that?"

"So I guess the answer is yes."

"More like fuck-buddies, but I did care about her a lot."

Jada took another swig and said, "Look, I'm not telling TeTe."

"She knows."

"How did she react?"

"She doesn't understand."

"That woman is cold."

"Exactly the reason I wanted to talk to you."

Jada crossed her arms.

"Have you heard from Mari?" Black asked.

Jada jumped up and retrieved her iPhone from her bedroom and said, "He left a number for you to call. He has a cell phone now."

"What?"

"Hey, he kept bugging me about getting him a cell phone and I was like what the hell? He has life so what can they do to him if they catch him?"

"You're right." Black removed his phone and punched Shamari's number in his phone.

Chapter 2

STARR TAPPED HER HEELS ON THE FLOOR OF Q'S penthouse. She sat on the sofa and Q was on an armchair with a cigar lit. His face was serious and calculating. Starr wanted to know what he was thinking, but she couldn't tell. There was an awkward silence. Starr felt bad that her nephew had stolen Q's product but she still couldn't help but blame him for what had happened. He was the one that had given the young man access to his home. He'd employed her nephew without even consulting her first.

Starr said, "I saw Meeka today."

"And what did she have say?"

"That she hadn't seen the boys in days."

"Did she say where my shit was?"

Starr looked upward. "Look, she didn't know anything about it."

"Did you tell her that her son is a goddamned thief?"

"At first I don't know if she believed it or not, but I think she knows now."

Q lit a cigar and blew a smoke ring. "Look, babe, I know I put you in a bad position."

Starr said, "I'm in a fucked-up position. One I didn't

choose to be in. I wish you would have asked me before you went behind my back and started communicating with DeMontre. How did you get in touch with DeMontre in the first place?"

He blew another smoke ring and she coughed and fanned the smoke away. She wished he would put that cigar out, but it was his house and she knew he could do what he damn well pleased.

"When you invited me to your mom's house for dinner, he asked me could he wash my cars for some extra bread so we exchanged numbers."

"Why didn't you let me know?"

"I don't know. It slipped my mind, I guess."

The disgusting smoke made her want to gag and when he realized that it bothered her, he stood and deposited it into the garbage disposal. When he returned to his seat he said, "Look, Starr. It's not like I'm going to hurt him, but I need to talk to him."

"I know, but he's my family. I can't let that go. He shouldn't have taken shit. And I'm going to get to the bottom of it."

She stood and marched toward the door and he said, "I have to tell you something."

She faced him. "What is it?"

"Naw. That's okay."

Her eyes were pleading. "What do you have to tell me? Did he do something else?"

"It's not about him."

"What is it about?"

"It's about us."

"Us. There is no us."

He gave her an empty stare.

"Look. I know I came over here the other day because I had heard about that girl and I shouldn't have let my emotions get the best of me."

"Your emotions got the best of you because you love me."

"I do." She batted her lashes. He licked his lips and she wanted to kiss them, but instead, she turned and he blocked the exit.

"Why are you doing this to me?"

"I have a confession."

"I don't have time for these silly-ass games, Quentin."

He smiled and the way she felt when she saw his smile affirmed that she loved this man so damn much.

"I never slept with Chanel."

"Huh?"

"I never slept with her."

"A little too old to be lying on your dick, ain't you?"

"Look, you asked me did I sleep with her and I said I did."

"Why?"

"I wanted to make you jealous."

"What?"

He pinned her hands to the wall door and attempted to kiss her but she dodged his lips. "You wanted to make me jealous? Why?"

"I dunno."

He released her hands and she shoved him. "You wanted to hurt me?"

"I hurt you?"

"You did."

"Why? You wanted to take a break."

"And you found a new girlfriend."

"I can't wait on you to make up your mind."

She said, "I know."

"What's wrong?"

"I don't know what's wrong." She avoided his eyes. "Part of me loves you and wants to be with you and knows that you can make me happy. But there are parts of me that don't feel right because I'm moving on so quickly. I loved Trey and for years Trey was all I knew and I sure as hell wasn't expecting to fall in love with one of his friends. And please don't say Trey is gone."

"No need for me to say that. You know that he's gone."

"I do."

"Are we going to keep ignoring our feelings?"

"Look, I need to find out where your dope is," she said. "Which brings me to another issue. You said that you were going to leave this alone. I don't want to bury another man."

"The drug game didn't kill Trey."

"I know, but it may well kill you."
"It's possible. It's life, and in life, you take chances."
"Goodbye, Q."

Chapter 3

BLACK LAY ACROSS HIS BED AND DIALED THE NUMBER THAT
Shamari had left for him. The voicemail picked up. Black didn't
want to leave a message. He simply texted, It's Black Boy.

Forty-five minutes later, Shamari called him back.

"I can't believe you got a phone."

"What can they do to me? I already got a life sentence."

"Exactly."

"What's up?" Shamari asked.

I don't know where to begin. I wish you were out here with
me dealing with this shit."

"What's wrong? I don't like hearing you sound like this."

"Did you see the news?"

"The news depresses me."

"The mayor's daughter committed suicide."

"Come see me. Next week. I really need to talk to you."

Black ended the call and seconds later he received a call
from Tara, L's baby mama. She was probably going to
be pissed that he missed the funeral. He answered the
phone anyway.

"Hey."

"I need to see you. "

"Is there something wrong?"

"Not really"

"Where are you?"

"I'm in Decatur. I'll text you my address."

Black arrived at Tara's apartment thirty minutes later. Tara was much prettier than Black expected her to be. She was a short petite woman with natural hair. Freckles sprinkled around her eyes and she had a pleasant smile.

"I finally get to meet the world famous Black."

"I'm not famous."

"I have fried chicken. You're welcome to it if you want."

"No, I'm good, Tara. I appreciate your offer. I wanna meet Latrell."

"You remember her name?"

"L loved that girl."

"He really did."

"How is she taking it?"

"Good days and bad days. The other day she asked when is God going to send daddy back down from heaven."

"Where is she?"

"With her grandma."

They sat in her tiny living room. The smell of fried chicken lingered in the air. Black's eyebrows squished together. She could tell he was confused.

She said, "I know what you're probably thinking."

"What am I thinking?"

"How did me and Larry meet?"

"I wasn't thinking that, but you can tell me the story if you want."

"That's not necessary, but most people want to know because he was so big and I'm so tiny."

"Opposites attract."

"They do. Plus L had a big heart. That's what attracted me to him. He was a kind man, but I hate that he played with my life like that."

"Huh?"

"Having sex with men."

"Oh." Black studied her face. She was a pleasant woman.

The kind of woman that wouldn't sleep around on you. was a hard worker and an excellent mother. She would attend PTA meetings with your kids, help with homework. She would be a team mom and bake cookies. She was that homely.

"So, why am I here?"

"You didn't come to the funeral."

Black glanced down at his hands. "I know and I'm sorry. I got arrested."

"I know."

"How did you know?"

"Detectives interviewed me. They said that they had you in custody. Asked me had I spoke with L the day that the triple homicide took place and I told them that he had visited Latrell and that you had picked him up that day."

"Oh, is that what you wanted to tell me?"

"No."

"What is it then?"

"Well, I have a phone number that I wanted to give you."

"Whose number is it?"

"The guy said his name was Bird. Said he had something that belonged to you."

"Bird? I don't know no motherfuckin' Bird."

"He came to Larry's funeral. He approached me and offered his condolences. Gave me a thousand dollars for Latrell and told me to get in touch with you."

Black was lost in thought wondering who the fuck was Bird. She passed him the number. It was an L.A. area code.

"How did Bird look?"

She laughed.

"What's so funny?"

"What's funny is Bird actually looks like a bird. Tall, gangly-looking guy. Sounded like he was from New York or California."

"New York and Cali accents sound nothing alike."

"All I know is that he ain't from Georgia."

Black laughed and said, "Tara, you seem like a good person."

"I try my best."

"Well, if you need anything, let me know."

"No, Black, if you need anything, you let me know. I mean

that. Although I don't know you that well, L loved you and I am the mother of L's daughter. If he loved you, I know you must be a good person."

"I try to be."

•   •   •

Black climbed inside his car, lowered the window a little and called Bird.

"Hello?"

"Bird?"

"Yeah."

"This is Black."

"I've been waiting on your call, homie."

California accent.

"What can I do for you?"

"I got something that you might want."

"First of all. How did you get my name in the first place?"

"I got something, or maybe someone, that you been looking for."

"What?"

"Avant. I have Avant."

"What?"

"Do you want him?"

"What do you want?"

"Give me fifty stacks and you can get him back."

"I don't give a damn about that clown. Keep him."

"But you do care?"

"What are you talking about?"

"He's organized a group of thugs and he's coming for your head, homie."

"Where do you want to meet?"

"There is a sports bar in Marietta called Mazzy's on Roswell."

"You going to be alone?"

"If you want."

"Give me an hour."

•   •   •

Somebody at the bar yelled, "Fuck the Dirty Birds." Monday Night Football was displayed on every plasma in Mazzy's. The Falcons and the Saints were playing and Julio Jones had just scored a touchdown—his second one of the night.

When Black walked into the place, he spotted Bird right away. He was a tall guy wearing an L.A. Dodgers ball cap, blue Chuck Taylors and a white tee with a blue bandana dangling from his back pocket. Bird had a long face with a long beak. His skin was the color of honey and he had exceptionally white teeth with a slight gap.

Black sat across from Bird. Bird snacked on barbecue chicken wings and was drinking a mug full of Bud Light.

Bird studied Black's face and said, "Do you drink?"

"Do you bang?"

"Used too. Rolling 40s, but I'm retired. Out here chasing paper but still always affiliated. You feel me?"

"You wanted to talk?"

"Look, homie, I'm going to keep it real with you. Your homie, L? We done that, but it was because he kicked in the door trying to turn up. You feel me? So we had to do what we had to do."

"I can understand that. So what about Avant?"

"They're going to get you."

"Do I look scared?"

"It ain't about being scared." Bird devoured one of those wings with one bite then licked the sauce from his finger. He noticed Black looking. He offered Black some wings.

Black plucked a couple from Bird's plate and placed them on the saucer in front of him.

"Look, I'm the one that went in your house and broke him out."

"How did you know where I lived?"

"Your boy had all that information on his phone. We wrote down the address then stuffed the phone back in his pocket before we dumped him on the side of the road."

Black thought back to the time when he had texted L his address. The first time he had come to his home.

"I don't get it. Why are you telling me this?"

A waiter named David approached the table. His hairy

belly was spilling from his T-shirt. He looked at Black and asked, "Can I get you something to drink?"

Black sent him on his way without ordering and then turned back to Bird. "Why are you telling me this?"

"Avant sent L to our house. This put us on the police's radar. The cops came in and kicked the door in a couple of days later. We had to move up out of there in a hurry."

"But L's body was found on the side of the road. Not at your house."

"We dumped him there. But someone heard the gunshots and police came in with a warrant saying that they received an anonymous tip saying that we were dealing out of the house. They came in looking for coke. The warrant was bogus. We don't sell coke."

Black made eye contact with Bird. "I'm going to ask you for the last time, why the fuck are you telling me all this?"

"You don't like the police. Me and you are alike."

"What did they find in the house?"

"A few plants and fifty thousand dollars. My homie Phil went to jail. We bailed him out the same night. Look, I'll bring you Avant if you give me fifty thousand dollars. He's out to get you, homie. No lie. He was talking to one of my homies about running up in some old lady's house."

Black remembered the day that he had bought Avant to Lani's mother, Ms. Carolyn's, house.

"Kill him. He made you lose the money, not me."

"But you want him."

"Not that bad."

Bird said. "Look, Black, there are gangstas from the West Coast that's mad about that money we lost and somebody is going to have to pay."

Black stared at Bird. "So you think you can scare me?"

"It ain't about being scared. It's about being smart. Look, I turn Avant over to you. You give me fifty thousand and I'll throw in six pounds of OG Kush. You can smoke it, sell it or whatever. You are not taking a loss."

"I'll think about it."

"You need to do more than think about it, homie. Shit can get real ugly around here for you."

Chapter 4

JADA'S DOORBELL RANG UNEXPECTEDLY. SHE WAS surprised to see Craig. How in the fuck did he know where she lived? She opened the door and said, "You get the hell away from my house right now or I'm calling the police."

"I need one moment."

"I'm supposed to help you? Get the fuck out of here. I'm going to call the police."

She stepped outside. A young white girl with a great tan, carrying a Pomeranian, looked at the two oddly as she passed by.

Jada said, "I will scream if you don't get the fuck away from here, you creep."

"Do you know how to get in touch with Cassandra?"

"Those are not my friends."

"Look, she has something that belongs to me."

"I'm sure."

"It's money."

"Money for tricking?"

"No."

"What the fuck am I even entertaining your dumb ass for? Craig, get the fuck away from me. I'm going to call the police."

"Look, I'm sorry."
"I don't ever want to see your ass again."
"Goodbye."

•   •   •

It was raining and the swishing of the windshield wipers made Black think of Lani. Jada had told him that she could no longer drive with wipers on. It reminded her of Lani's last moments and it was too much for her to handle.

He was happy he hadn't been the one talking on the phone with her when she was murdered. He was sure it would be too much for him to handle too and it still was. There was no denying it that he was the reason that Lani and L were both dead. He traced an imaginary cross over his heart and said, "Lani, I miss you so much."

He whipped into a gas station parking lot. Seconds later, a black Jeep Grand Cherokee pulled in right beside him.

The man presented Black with an F.B.I. badge and said, "I'm Special Agent Barry Daniels."

Black examined the badge. "So what you want with me?"

Daniels laughed.

"What's so funny?"

"Can we talk for a moment?"

"I don't talk to cops."

"Listen to me."

"Talk."

"Trust me. You're going to want to hear me out."

Black laughed. "I told you. I don't talk to cops."

"I want to do business and I want to give you a license to do business in Atlanta."

"I am already a businessman."

"You know what I mean."

"No I don't."

"I can get you all the product you need and it will be between you and me."

"What are you saying?"

"I'm saying, I work for the Feds and you're a drug dealer. I can get what you want—if you trust me."

"What do I want?"

Daniels approached Black and said, "Look, bruh, I know the streets want coke and the Mexicans are the only ones with access. I have access and I say that me and you work together."

"You think I'm going to work with you?"

"You got two choices, Black."

"And they are?"

"You work with me and I make this Homeland Security investigation go away. Or you do it on your own and you'll be indicted within six months. I happen to know they are close to putting your black ass away for life. They are building a case on you."

There was a long silence as Black studied Daniel's face. This was crazy. Like some shit he'd seen in a movie.

"What would be my take if I work with you?"

"I'll work something out real nice for you. Better than you can find anywhere."

Black stared up. "How do you even know me?"

"You were Sasha Anderson's boyfriend. I saw you at the hotel the other day when her body was found. Your girlfriend killed herself." Daniels said.

"Okay."

"She was trying to bring her pops down."

"Mayor Anderson."

"Yeah."

"So what's going to happen to him?" Black asked.

"He's going to step down. I make his charges go away. He resigns. Everybody is happy."

"So it was you that told him that he was being investigated?"

"Look, I'm not going to go into specifics of what happened. Black, you're a drug dealer. You're not going to stop dealing and I'm the Feds. Let me make your life easier."

"And be my supplier? I can get killed if anybody finds out."

"And I can go to prison for a long time. Black, you trust me and I trust you."

"This goes against everything that I ever stood for."

"Black, I'm from the hood. I know the struggle...brother."

Black studied his face. He looked serious. He didn't look

lame. The motherfucker actually looked street smart.
  "You'll make the Homeland Security shit go away?"
  "Disappear."
  "How?"
  "Don't worry about that.""
  "Shamari Brooks?"
  "You want him out?"
  "Yeah."
  "I'll see what I can do."
  "Okay."
  "Did he tell you that he's been getting visits from them?"
  "No."
  "Don't worry. He's loyal to you."
A streak of lightning shot across the sky and the rain started coming down harder. Then there was thunder.
  Daniels thumped the cigarette onto the pavement then stomped it out. "Let me know what you're going to do." Then he passed Black a card.
  "But what if I tell your higher ups that you came to me with that proposition?"
  "You won't."
  "How can you be so sure?"
  "Those dirty white boys that picked you up about a month ago. They'll be back, but this time they'll end your life."
  "Huh?"
  "Yeah. Those were my boys."
  "But why did you send them to hurt me?"
  "The mayor thought you were getting too close. Influencing Sasha. It was a favor and that's when I sent them after you."

Chapter 5

Brooke was face-timing with her best friend Michelle who was studying in France. Her feet were kicked up and she was snacking on almonds when Starr tapped her on the shoulder. Brooke turned and faced her.

Starr said, "When you're done, I need to see you in my office."

"Am I in trouble?"

"No."

Five minutes later Brooke entered Starr's office and sat across from Starr's desk and said, "Hey, I apologize for face-timing, but you know I don't see my friend that often—"

Starr cut her off. "That's not an issue for me. Nobody was in the studio. I don't have a problem with that."

"What is it?"

"Have you seen DeMontre?"

Brooke avoided Starr's eyes.

"You've never lied to me."

"I haven't seen him but I have talked to him. As a matter of fact, he texted a couple of hours ago. What's wrong?"

"He and his brother have been missing for a few days."

"Does this have anything to do with the money that he took from Mr. Q?"

"How did you know about that?"

Brooke tried to ease away from Starr but Starr jumped in front of her.

"I met up with DeMontre to give him the handbag back and he cursed me out," Brooke said.

"Why did you give it back?" Starr asked.

"My mom made me give it back."

"So you've seen him?"

"A few days ago."

"I thought you hadn't seen him?"

"I thought you meant today."

"Come on, Brooke, you knew what I meant."

Brooke ran her fingers through her hair. Starr could tell she was holding something in. "Do you have something you want to tell me?"

"He's going to be pissed at me."

"Look, I don't give a damn, little girl. I'll go tell your mom that you've still been in contact with the little thug that bought you the bag."

"Look, I know where he is. His brother is with him."

"Tell me."

"DeMontre texted me this address a few days ago. The day I went to see him."

"Whose house is it?"

"It's a trap house."

"So you've been hanging out in a trap house?"

"I was only there for a few hours."

"A few hours is too much. Do you know that you could have gone to jail or got murdered?"

"I know. I didn't go back."

Starr had told Q the whereabouts of DeMontre and shortly after Fresh had called Q to apologize for kicking him out of his house earlier. Q still wasn't happy that Fresh had decided to work with Diego but he accepted the apology. He loved Fresh and recruited him to help find DeMontre, but they weren't from Atlanta and Fresh's cousin was a square, so they decided to bring Black along because they needed him. He knew Atlanta and Fresh wanted to work with him again since the murder charges had been dropped. Black led them straight to the address. Black's friend Big Ced lived on the next street over. Black called Big Ced as soon as they pulled into the hood. Fresh parked a few feet away from the small, dilapidated house. Beer cans and cigarette butts decorated the dirt yard.

"You know whose house is this?"

Ced said, "A crackhead ho named Dianne."

"They must have paid her."

"So, what's the deal? Why are we here?" Ced asked.

Black said, "Lookin' for a little motherfucker that stole from us."

"You gotta kill him." Ced said.

"We can't." Black said.

"Why not?"

"It's his girl's nephew." Black pointed to Q.

"I would still kill him."

"She would never forgive me." Q said.

"And I would never forgive her for introducing me to the little thieving-ass nigga. Motherfuckers have died for way less than that."

"We can't kill him."

"Oh. So why are we here?"

"To scare him up a bit."

"Knock on the door." Fresh said to Black.

"This ain't my hood and this ain't my shit. I'm here for back up, but that's it."

Ced said, "I'll do it."

Q said, "I'll go with you."

They banged on the door and someone inside the house let off a round. Ced and Q dove off the side of the porch and crawled to the side of the house.

The door flew open. DeVante, DeMontre and another teen named Marco sprinted outside firing their guns. Black and Fresh ducked behind the car and the teens chased them, firing shots. The car window shattered as Black crawled under the car and prayed to God that he didn't get hit.

Ced crept up behind DeMontre and took hold of his neck. "Drop the guns or I'm smokin' his ass."

DeVante said, "Drop em."

Ced looked like an insane man. The whites of his eyes displayed. He didn't give a fuck about them. They had tried to assassinate him. The three weapons clanked on the dirt.

Q appeared from the side of the house. Black and Fresh sprung to their feet.

Q approached DeMontre and slapped the fuck out him and said, "Where the hell is my shit?"

"I don't know what you're talking about."

DeVante said, "Don't hit my brother."

Black snatched his little ass off the ground and was

choking the fuck out of him when crackhead Dianne came to the door. She had salt and pepper braids that wrapped around her oval face. She had teeth the color of corn. She was wearing some dingy jeans and a dirty brown T-shirt and was barefoot. "Ced, what the hell is going on?"

"Mind yo goddamned business, Dianne."

"I'm calling the police if you don't tell me what's going on."

Ced fired a shot and pierced the top of Dianne's hair. "The next bullet is going through your forehead."

Q said to DeMontre, "Motherfucker, do you think I'm something to play with? Huh?"

"Look, man, I'm sorry."

"Where is my shit?"

"I don't have it."

"What did you do with it?"

"I sold it."

"Where the fuck is the money?"

"All I got is eight bands."

"Where is it?"

"He's lying, bruh," Ced said.

"I swear to God, bruh. That's all I got."

Ced jammed the gun down DeMontre's throat. His brother shook uncontrollably.

"Please! Don't do it!" Then he made eye contact with Q. "Uncle Q, don't let him kill my brother."

"Somebody better tell me something."

Q made eye contact with Black, his facial expression saying why in the hell did you bring this lunatic out here?

The other twin said to Black, "I'll give you the work and the money. Don't hurt my brother."

Black said, "Where the fuck is it then." His gun still aimed at Twin's head.

"It's in the car."

"What car?"

He pointed to a blue Ford Fusion.

Black grabbed him by the shirt and led him over to the car and ordered him to open the trunk. Sitting in the trunk was a brick of coke and eighteen thousand dollars.

"This is all we got, bruh. I swear to God."

Black laughed and said to Q, "What you want to do?"

"Let's get that."

Ced shoved DeMontre to the ground and kicked him in the ribs. "You lucky it ain't my shit."

Chapter 6

Tank presented the clerk his Gold American Express card to pay for the hotel suite at the Ritz Carlton. Jada had made it clear that if she was going to play the side chick and didn't know where he resided, then she was not going to let him know where she resided. Not yet.

She lay in bed with him, plucking French fries from his room service tray.

"I can't allow you to force me to pay for a room and you have a place." Tank said.

She frowned said, "Is that how you see it? I forced you to buy a room?"

"I pay for furniture and movers. I should at least be allowed to crash at your place."

"You will. But not right now."

"So who is he, Jada?"

"Who is who?"

"My competition."

"You ain't worried are you? Do I look like I'm losing sleep over that country-ass girlfriend of yours?"

"I'm not worried."

"I actually have no idea what you mean."

"Who is the lucky man?"

"You the lucky man for the night." She plucked more of his fries and dabbed them in the puddle of ketchup.

"Why do women always take food off men's plates?"

Jada rolled her eyes and said, "Aren't we petty?"

"Not petty. It's an observation."

"I guess we want to know that what's yours is ours."

He laughed and said, "I like you, Jada. You are something else."

She caressed his chest and said, "You think so?"

"I know so." He inched toward her then pecked her lips. "You saw something that you wanted and you went for it."

She forced a smile and her face tightened. "I saw something that I wanted? Nigga, you're the one that doubled back and left your woman to talk to me."

"And here we are."

"Yup." She leaned into him and they kissed.

He cupped her breast and said, "Implants?"

"Yeah, you don't like it?"

"I do."

"You sure?"

"I'm from Miami. Everybody has fake parts down there."

"What about your girl?"

"No."

"Well then, everybody doesn't."

"Nothing wrong with a little enhancement." He patted her on the ass and said, "That's real. I can tell."

"Yup. It shole is," she lied. He didn't need to know she'd had that enhanced too.

"Shole. Is that a word?"

"In Georgia it is." She laughed.

"So who is the lucky man?"

"Let's not talk about him."

"There is a him?"

"Is there a her?"

"You seen her."

"And she wasn't much to look at."

"Oh that was cold, Jada."

"We fucking or what?"

He removed the blue boxer briefs and his dick stood erect. It was short, but thick and powerful looking. He had shredded abs, broad shoulders and a nice ass himself. She was curious if Mr. Tank knew what he was doing.

She lay on her back and touched her kitty as he made his way to the bed and dove between her legs. His tongue traced her navel and then traveled down to her inner thighs. Then he placed his lips on her clit. He was kind of hesitant and she nudged him. Her hairless kitty smelled like cotton candy.

She squirmed. His tongue felt so damn good inside her.

She took hold of his shoulders and pulled him up to her and said, "I want you inside. Do you have a condom?"

"I do."

"Get it."

He jumped up and walked to his pants which were across the room folded on a chair. He dug in his wallet for the magnum and seconds later, he was back in the bed with the condom on.

His hard dick grazed her leg. "I want you."

When he penetrated her, she screamed. "God, you feel so good!" Her hands on his ass bringing him closer. Her tongue fucked the inside of his earlobe, arousing him further.

He flipped her on her side and spooned her as she pinched her rigid nipples.

He watched his dick go in and out of her love hole. And finally, he turned her over on her back. She loved the way he took charge and manhandled her. Tank was indeed a man that could handle her.

He yanked her hair and for a second she thought about having just gone to the salon until he said, "Look at me, slut."

She usually had to instruct guys that it was okay to insult her and even then, they didn't want too.

He yanked her hair again and said, "Look at me, slut."

"I'll do whatever you want." She held onto her left breast as Tank kept grinding.

She said, "Call me slut again."

He flipped her over and started fucking her missionary style while he choked her. Suddenly, she erupted and seconds later he discharged.

They lay in the bed and he rolled over on his stomach and grabbed one of those cold-ass French fries from the room-service tray. He chomped it down and said, "Jada, I feel a connection."

"Huh?"

"This. What we have. Was meant to be."

"And what about country?"

"Who is country?"

"Your lady."

"What?"

"That's my nickname for her because she sure as hell looked country when I saw her."

He laughed. He faced her and said, "Jada, I enjoy your company. I want more."

She didn't know how to respond. She sprang from the bed and headed to the bathroom to pee.

Chapter 7

Fresh and Q were headed to Q's condo. J Cole's No Role Models was playing on the radio.

Fresh lowered the volume of the radio and said, "I wanna ask you something that has been on my mind."

Q's face was serious. "What is it?"

"Did you wanna have Trey murdered?"

Q sighed and glanced out the window, avoiding Fresh's eyes. Q turned to face Fresh without saying anything.

"You don't have to lie to me. I didn't know Trey that well. He was your guy, not mine."

"I asked Diego to send a team up here to murder him."

"But he was your friend."

"He was."

"Trey had seen me and he got pulled in Louisiana with a shitload of coke and they let him go."

"You thought he was an informant?"

"I didn't know. So I couldn't take any chances."

"So you were going to knock him off?"

"I was. Not because I wanted to. But it's the business, you know?"

"So why did he say they let him go?"

"Said some bullshit about the cop wanted the money that he had."

"What money?"

"The day Trey came to see me. I couldn't fill his whole order so I sent him back with half the order and he took his money with him."

"So he got pulled with money and coke?"

"Yeah."

Fresh pulled into Q's building. Q passed him the FOB to get into the parking deck.

When they were parked, the conversation continued. Fresh said, "So you don't think what he was saying is possible?"

"I don't know."

"Let me tell you, cops want money like the rest of us. I think it's possible. Get one of these lowlifes from one of these hick towns. They'll accept a bribe, man."

"You think so?"

"It's happened before. It happened to me."

"You never told me that."

"If I told you, would you have believed me?"

There was a brief silence before Q said, "Probably not."

"That's fucked up, Q."

"Look, he's gone anyway and I didn't have shit to do with it."

"But you wanted the man dead, and you're fucking his wifey."

• • •

Over lobster and Hennessy, TeTe introduced Black to Eli as her former boyfriend. Black looked confused. How did this woman have the audacity to introduce him to her ex-boyfriend? Black shook Eli's hands and noticed one of his fingers were missing. He said it was a long story, but Black knew the story. He had forgotten, but she had told him once they'd made love that she'd chopped Eli's finger off. He thought she was kidding but it appears that the bitch was, in fact, being truthful. Black pulled TeTe into the den away from Eli.

And when the door closed, Black said, "What the fuck is this all about?"

"What is what all about?"

"You introducing me to your old dick."

TeTe sat her drink down and said, "Look that was a long time ago." She lied. She sucked him a few days ago, but Black didn't need to know that.

"That's not a good idea."

"I don't belong to either of you."

"I love you."

"And I love you. Why do you think I flipped out when I found out that you were helping that suicidal bitch?"

"My friend."

"Eli is gonna tell us where Todd is."

"What?"

"Todd and some Detroit dudes came over to Eli's place a few weeks ago asking Eli all kinds of questions about me and my daughter."

"The same dudes that Champagne told me about?"

"Who?"

"The stripper."

TeTe's hand rested on her hip and said, "To think you have the fucking nerve to tell me what I should and shouldn't be doing."

"I ain't fuck her."

"Whatever." She picked up her drink and downed it. She turned to walk back into the kitchen when Black slapped her ass.

She said, "Don't start with me."

"I don't give a damn that he's here."

"Me, either."

In the kitchen, Eli filled Black in on all the things that he'd told TeTe. That the Detroit boys wanted information about TeTe and Butterfly.

Black said to Eli, "Where does Todd live?"

"I don't know."

"We have to find him."

Black thought about Cato. He hadn't heard from him. He would have to contact some of his partners from his old hood. Get in touch with his mom to find out if she heard from him. He'd been calling his phone for the last few days but it went straight to voice mail. His first order of business was to find Todd's whereabouts.

TeTe's phone rang.

"Hello."

There was screaming and hollering on the phone.

TeTe said, "Honey, you're going to have to calm down and tell me what happened. Who hit you? Why? He tried to choke you? You hit him with one of your heels? I'll be there in a second."

TeTe terminated the call. "We have to go. One of my girls is in trouble."

"Which one?" Eli asked.

"The tranny."

"I'll go with you." Black said.

Eli said, "We'll both go."

TeTe tapped on room 1824 of the W Hotel. Black, TeTe and Eli stormed the plush hotel suite. Miss America sat on the edge of the bed sobbing and TeTe approached her.

"Okay, you want to explain to me how you ended up with Dr. Matthews? You were supposed to see a new customer."

"He lied like he was somebody else and when I came in the room only then did I realize that he had lied and pretended to be someone else. You're the one that scheduled the appointment."

TeTe scratched her head. "I didn't pick up on the voice."

"I swear I thought I was meeting someone else."

"So where the fuck is my money, bitch?"

Miss America dug into her purse and passed TeTe the thousand dollars.

TeTe stared at the money. "Where is the rest of the goddamned money?"

"He only wanted conversation, remember?"

TeTe laughed. "I totally forgot."

"But I didn't get paid."

"What do you mean?"

"Well, he knew that if he didn't pay you, there would be consequences, so he paid me the half that was due to you and he said that he wasn't going to give me shit because I knew where Cassandra was."

Black said. "Fy-Head?"

"Yes."

"What does she have to do with it?"

TeTe said, "I'm about sick of this dude. Something has to be done about him now."

"Who?" Black asked.

"Weird-ass doctor that used to fuck Jada."

Black said, "Oh, I know exactly who you're talking about. What happened?"

Miss America said, "He wanted his wife murdered. Cassandra said she would help him but she and this dude named J-Will accepted the money without doing the job."

"And what happened?"

"Nothing happened. He thinks I know where she is and he tried to attack me and choke me but I slapped him with my high-heel shoe. Hotel security came and asked me was everything okay."

TeTe was pacing. She was furious and she dialed his phone number but he didn't answer. She dialed the number again and this time it went straight to voicemail.

TeTe embraced Miss America and passed the money to her. "Here, take the money and go home. Get some rest. I'll catch up with him."

●   ●   ●

Craig lay in bed situated between two naked nineteen-year-old male escorts. Tall, lean, hairless sensational-looking fitness models. The two escorts took turns jerking him off. There was no penetration and for this reason Craig felt he wasn't gay. An eight ball of pure coke was positioned on the dresser.

The door to the bedroom crashed open and there stood Black, Eli and TeTe. The escorts bounced up from the bed butt naked with their dicks swinging wildly. This was more than Black wanted to see. Craig tried to make a dash for the bathroom.

TeTe pointed her pink .380 at him and said, "Stop because if I fire this gun, it's going to blow your fuckin' heart out."

Black said, "Can you let these dudes cover up?" Black tossed the dudes some bed covers.

Craig threw his hands up and said, "What the hell is going on?"

"You tell me."

"She's been paid."

"But you made an appointment under an alias."

"What difference does it make? I paid the new client fee with my credit card and I gave her the rest of the money."

"This is not how shit works around here. A—you don't set your own prices and B—you don't treat my girls like shit and C—didn't your mama tell you not to put your hands where they don't belong and D—you lied about who the fuck you were."

TeTe turned to Eli. "Restrain him." Then she faced the two male escorts and said, "Sit these two sissies right here on the floor."

Black snatched Craig's ass up. He kicked and squirmed until Eli restrained him. TeTe removed a tube of Superglue from her purse and applied glue to the palm of his hands and then attached them to his bare balls.

"Where the fuck is my money?"

"You've been paid."

She whacked him with the butt of the gun and said, "Where is the money?"

"I don't have any money."

She passed Black the glue and said, "Glue this motherfucker's lips shut."

"There is money on the dresser," one of the escorts said. "Don't kill us."

TeTe moseyed her way over to the dresser and counted the money. It was four thousand dollars.

"Hey, I only owe you fifteen hundred."

"You're going to have to pay me for my time, bitch."

Black and Eli tossed his ass in the air like he was a kettle bell and with his hands super glued to his balls, there was no way he could break his fall. He crashed face first.

Chapter 8

Starr was skimming through old invoices, alone in the studio when she was interrupted by Q entering the studio.

She said, "I'm disappointed in you."

"Me?"

"Yes."

"What I do?"

"Jamming a gun down my nephew's throat!"

"Calm down. First of all. I didn't put anything in your nephew's mouth. One of Black's friend's did that."

Starr sighed heavily. "You let it happen."

"Starr, shit don't happen to people. He did that to himself. So what did he do? Go whining to his auntie? Did he tell you that they fired a round at us as soon as they saw us? Hell, we had to run for cover."

"You could have killed him."

"And he could have killed us. I didn't let anything happen to him."

She crossed her arms and said, "He's still a kid."

"He's a kid, but you know, he should be dead right now."

"I know and I'm so sorry about that. I really am."

"No worries."

"So what brings you here?"

"I was in the neighborhood and thought I would stop by."

"For what?"

"I missed you."

"Where is your girlfriend?"

"I don't know where she is."

"So she is your girlfriend?"

"No, but that's what you call her."

He approached Starr and caressed her neck. His fingers grazing her earlobe and then he pulled her into him. She rested her head against his chest and he pecked her on the forehead. His hands seized her waist and traveled down and took hold of her ass.

She smiled. "I know you think I'm crazy, don't you?"

"I don't know. We both might be a little crazy, but I don't know why I keep coming back to you. For some reason, I can't stop thinking about you."

"Well, I'm not going to ask you to get out of the game."

Their eyes locked. "Look, that day is coming."

"When they lower you in the ground."

"That will never happen."

"I lost one man."

"The game didn't kill him."

"But the game could have."

Q thought about the fact that Fresh knew that he had wanted Trey murdered.

"I'm not your mother. You can do whatever you want." Starr said.

"But I'll never have you."

She turned her back and tried to ease away. He took hold of her shoulder and spun her around.

"We can never live together." Starr said.

"Why?"

"You know why."

"I don't love her. I love you."

"You do?"

He smiled and her heart skipped a beat as she made eye contact with this gorgeous man. Why couldn't he be a good guy? Then everything would be perfect, she thought.

But she knew that if he was a good guy, she wouldn't want him. She was no better than Brooke wanting her nephew to change. In fact, she was more pathetic than Brooke. She was a grown woman and she still loved the bad guys.

He yanked her into him and he unbuttoned her blouse.

She said, "No," but she meant yes, keep going.

He cupped her ass, massaging it.

She closed her eyes and said, "Oh, God."

"Oh, God, is right."

He placed her hand on his rock-solid tool. She felt it pulsating. She broke free from his grip and scurried across the room to lock the showroom.

When she approached him, she said to herself, "What am I doing? What the hell am I doing?"

He hoisted her up and made his way over to a brown leather sofa in the show room.

She protested and he looked confused. "What's wrong?"

"Who fucks on leather?"

He laughed and he snatched her up. He transported her over to the sofa. Damn, she felt secure with him. The only man that she wanted.

He lay her down and removed her skirt revealing lace panties. He removed his pants and admired her body at the same time. Although they'd had sex a few times before, he was still very much in awe of her fantastic figure.

He dropped his underwear and his dick was now erect—long, lean, and powerful. She sprang from the sofa.

"Where you going?"

"To get a blanket from my office."

"What?"

"I don't feel right with my bare ass on this sofa, sir. I still got to sell this stuff."

"Clean it. Hell, I'll pay for it."

She giggled and disappeared into the back. Moments later, she returned with a slipcover. He couldn't stop smiling as he plopped back down on the sofa.

He forced her on her back as he inched his way up to her thighs and pecked away. His tongue circled her kitty and she wanted to scream, "Fuck me right now!" She brushed his hair with her fingers, her nails tickling his scalp.

"Fuck me now."

"Not yet." he said.

"What's wrong?"

"Not fully hard."

She sat up on the sofa. "Let me help you."

He positioned himself until he was sitting up on the sofa. She took him inside her mouth and tugged at his balls until he came alive in her mouth. She then positioned her body while still standing until he was able to infiltrate her. He doggy-styled her until they were exhausted and eventually fell back on the sofa. They fucked until he brought her to multiple orgasms. After having sex with Q several times, she had concluded that his appeal wasn't his lovemaking skills, though they were good, but the fact that she loved the man. He grunted before coming inside her just as the couch collapsed.

And she said, "Looks like you're going to have to buy the sofa after all."

"Not a problem." He stood up, his dick swinging. Her eyes fixated on his ass and that chiseled abdomen. He asked, "Is there a shower here?"

"I'm sorry, sir, I don't have a shower. I never imagined I'd be having sex in my showroom."

"You never know what might happen when you're with me."

"I see. I have a sink in the back and some towels."

"Towels? Towels for after sex?"

"No silly. There are two women that work here."

"Let's clean up then head to my place for round two."

"You ain't ready for all of that."

Chapter 9

Brooke parked her BMW in front of the trap house and blew her horn. DeVante opened the door and ducked back inside and said, "Hey, bruh. That black-white girl outside."

"Who?"

"You know? Your little shawty that works for Auntie Starr."

DeMontre sat at the kitchen and was chopping crack cocaine with a razor blade into itty-bitty pieces.

"You want me to invite her in?"

"Naw. Come finish doing this."

Marco was leaning over cleaning his Jordan's with a toothbrush and soap. He said, "I don't know why you hanging with that little bitch in the first place. She don't want to fuck. All she want to do is cuddle with yo ass, and I'm sure she was the one that told your auntie where you was in the first place."

"Old cuddling-ass nigga."

DeVante and Marco laughed their asses off as DeMontre left the house.

DeMontre approached the car and said, "So what are you doing over here, shawty?"

"I came to make sure you were all right."

"Well, I'm all right."

"Get in the car."

He scanned the area before hopping into the car. Drake's Back to Back was playing on the radio.

"I missed you."

He chuckled and she asked, "What's so funny?"

"Shawty, you got my brother and 'em clowning me."

"For what?"

"Because we haven't done it."

"What do you mean?"

"Don't play dumb. You know what I mean."

"Because we haven't had sex?"

"Damn, you smart. I guess they do teach you a lot at that rich school."

"Quit being sarcastic."

"Shawty, what do you want?"

"I want you. I want to be with you."

"You snitched on me, shawty. You told my auntie exactly where I was at."

There was an awkward silence. A crackhead named Billy tapped on her window and startled her. She jumped and he laughed.

Billy grinned, revealing missing front teeth and said. "Baby girl, I ain't gonna bother you. I was wanting to know if you wanted to buy a computer."

DeMontre said, "Let the window down."

She lowered the window and the crackhead said, "I'm sorry, nephew. You wanna buy a computer?"

"Take it in the house and show it to my brother."

He grinned again and said, "Nephew, she a banger." Then he gave DeMontre a thumbs up.

When she let the window back up, he said, "Me and you are from different worlds, shawty."

"What does that mean?"

"It means it is what it is."

"I think you and your brother should go home."

"For what? Ain't nothing there for me. My mama don't give a fuck where I'm at."

"I think you're wrong about that. I overheard her saying that she wants y'all—"

"Shawty, you don't know nothing about my life."

"You right and I'm sorry. I'm sorry I told your auntie where you were."

"You could have gotten me killed."

"I know."

"Is there anything else you want to tell me?"

"I love you and I've been thinking about what you asked me to do. I think I want to do it."

"I thought you wanted to be a virgin until you got married?"

"I did until I met you."

"So when you want to do it?"

"We can do it this weekend."

He smiled. "You nervous?"

"I am a little."

"I won't hurt you…I promise." He leaned into her and kissed her.

Chapter 10

Shamari rested his elbows on the table inside the visitation room listening intently as Black explained to him about Sasha's suicide. He explained to him how she was going to make a deal with the Feds to bring her father down and to try to get him out of prison.

"Look, the Feds tried to get me to tell them something about you. I didn't do it and I'd remembered you saying something about some government corruption in the mayor's office, so I told them to go see her."

"So you sent them to her?"

"Yeah. I thought it might help me."

"Okay. They told me."

"Who told you?"

"Well, there this dude, man, he's a F.B.I. agent. He wants me to sell coke for him. You know I really don't know what to do."

"What the fuck you mean he wants you to sell for him?"

"I don't know what the deal is, man. I think he's like taking shit from dope boys and putting it back on the streets. I don't want to do it though."

"So how does this work?"

"He wants to split the profits with me—fifty/fifty."

"Don't do it."

"I'm not. I got some other shit that I'm working on, but dude is telling me that Homeland Security wants me bad."

"They want you, bruh."

"I know."

There was an awkward silence then Shamari said, "So have you seen Jada?"

"I spoke with her a few days ago. She doing good."

"Look, I have a confession."

"What?"

"I really did think that you were fuckin Jada."

"I know you did. A lot of people think I'm grimy but I'll never be grimy to my friends. And absolutely not to a brother and you're like a brother to me."

"I appreciate you, man."

Black stood and Shamari rose from his seat. They embraced and Shamari said to Black, "I gotta get out of here, man. I don't wanna die in here."

"I'm going to try my best."

•　•　•

When Todd went into the garage and saw the big black gun with the silencer pointed at his dome, he screamed. "What do you want? Money?"

Black said, "You're coming with me, pussy!"

Eli and TeTe drove up in a conversion van and Eli and Black tossed Todd in the back of the van. They then sped off to one of TeTe's home's in Riverdale, Georgia.

Two unidentified goons stripped Todd butt naked and hog-tied him. He was lying in the middle of the floor squirming.

TeTe said, "So, what do you want to tell me?"

"About what?"

Todd was a fairly intelligent guy and it didn't take much to figure out that he was going to die unless he could somehow talk himself out of this compromising situation.

"Hey, I was going to find you today."

"Really? How was you going to find me and why was you

going to find me?”

“I wanted to apologize because I knew I kind of lost it a little bit when I found out what happened to Dank.”

“I told you, I don’t know what happened to Dank.” TeTe was lying because she knew damn well that she was the one that ran Dank’s ass over and brutally crushed his skull.

“And I believe you.”

“Is that why you were making plans for revenge with Shakur’s brothers?”

Todd looked at Eli. “So is that what Eli told you?”

“You’re a goddamn traitor.”

Todd was in excruciating pain caused by the way he was hog-tied. Todd pleaded with TeTe. ”Can you at least let me go to the bathroom? I have to pee.”

TeTe laughed. “Do you really think I give a fuck that you got to pee?”

She dropped her pants, revealing her naked ass so that everyone in the room could see. She cocked her ass over Todd’s face and said, “I have to pee too.”

Eli was staring hard and Black slapped the fuck out of him.

“What are you doing, babe?”

“I’m pissing on this dirt bag.”

She sprayed Todd face’s with urine as he squirmed on the floor.

TeTe pulled her pants up and Black was disgusted by his pretty little princess that was now cleaning her kitty with a feminine wipe.

“You betrayed me.”

“I’m sorry.”

TeTe said to Black, “Give me the gun.”

“No, not now.”

“What?”

“I want him to tell us where the Detroit boys are.”

“Kill me right now. I know you’re going to do it anyway.”

“You’re going to tell us.”

“I was introduced to them through a stripper.”

“Sapphire?”

“You know I did and that’s why you sent your boy to kill me.”

"What boy?"

"Short dude. Think she said his name was Cato."

"How do you know that?"

"It had to be you. Who else would want me dead?"

"Where is Cato?"

"Is there anything you want me to tell him?"

"What do you mean?"

"He's dead. I guess I'll be seeing him in a few."

"What? You murdered my friend?" Black lowered his head and swallowed hard.

"I had no choice."

TeTe doused lighter fluid on his legs and lit it. He screamed. "Oh, God, God! Please, please, Lord, Lord! God help me!" Todd screamed as the smell of burning human flesh permeated through the place.

Black sat down on the carpet. His head between his legs. Cato was dead and though they weren't as close as they were growing up, he was the reason for this death too.

Todd was still screaming. "Please, put the fire out! I'll take you to the Detroit boys."

TeTe said, "You can pee now if you want to."

Chapter 11

Jada stood in front of Lennox mall waiting on the valet to bring her car when a girl approached her.

"Hey, what's your name?" the girl asked.

She was a cute girl. She had a nice body but a bit too athletic for Jada's taste. Nice hair and smile but she needed to get rid of those country-ass Steve Madden wedges. Jada would give her an eight for her appearance.

Jada removed her sunglasses to see if she recognized the girl. "I'm Aimee." Jada lied. The bitch didn't need to know her name. For all she knew, she could have been friends with Tank's wifey.

"Aren't you friend's with Starr?"

"Yeah. Why?"

"My name is Shantelle. We fought at Trey's funeral. Well, you beat my ass."

"Oh, so you back for more?"

"Can we talk?"

"Look, I'm sorry for what happened. I'm really trying to change my life around."

"No worries."

"So, what's up?"

"I seen Starr a few months ago with Q and they were leaving a restaurant together. I didn't know that he had moved up here."

"So you're trying to move in on Q too?"

"Oh hell, no. Not at all."

"So what's it to you that she was seeing Q?"

"She's not any longer?"

"You know how it can be off and on. I'm sure you done that with a dude a time or two."

She laughed and said, "I have but I'm a big girl now. Thirty plus, so if marriage ain't in the plans, he can go the hell on."

The valet pulled Jada's car up.

"Hey, I gotta go. Good seeing you."

"Look, I really want to talk to you." She dug into her purse and removed a twenty-dollar bill and said, "Pay the valet. Tell him to leave the car out front."

Jada ordered the valet to park the car on the side.

"So what's on your mind? I really have to go."

"Look, I don't think Starr knows everything there is to know about Q."

"What do you mean?"

"Q is not a good guy."

"What do you mean?" Jada said. Then she sat her bags on the ground and said, "Didn't you run off with Trey's money?"

"I split the money with his baby mama."

"Ok, you're kind of scandalous too, shawty."

"I loved Trey."

"You loved his money."

She smirked and said, "Let me tell you what happened."

Jada's hands rested on her hips. "I'm waiting."

"Look, me and Trey got pulled over in Louisiana with drugs in the car and the police took the money and let us go."

"Ok."

"A few weeks later, I was jogging in my neighborhood and a van full of Mexicans pulled up beside me and threw me in the van. They take me to this location and when I get there, I see Q and he questions me about what happened when we got pulled. Asked me if Trey was snitching. Basically, he didn't believe the story I told him."

"So is that why you took the money?"

"I took the money because I needed it."

"Why did you need it?"

"Because Q told me that they was going to kill me."

"Kill you for what?"

"He wanted me to bring Trey to him and the Mexicans and they were going to kill him, but I didn't. I may have took the money and I was never in love with Trey, but I loved him."

"So you're saying that Q wanted Trey dead?"

"That's exactly what I'm saying."

"Understandable. He's a drug lord and he thought Trey was snitching."

"Look, I was just telling you. I don't mean to cause any problems and please don't tell nobody that I told you this."

"I won't." Jada embraced her.

Jada said, "Put my number in your phone. You seem like a pretty cool chick."

"I am." She sighed and said, "I'm just a girl that loves the wrong men."

"Ain't that all our problems?"

"And I'm sorry about what happened to your friend."

"Huh?"

"I think her name was Lani or something like that?"

"How did you know what happened to her?"

"I follow you on Instagram. I saw you post up the message that you hate the rain and you hate wipers because it reminds you so much about what happened with Lani. The first time I saw you, Starr and Lani was when you came to Atlantic Station and you all wanted to jump me. Y'all seemed pretty close."

"Yeah, Lani was my best friend."

"She was Starr's best friend, too?"

"Yeah, Lani introduced me and Starr."

"Are you going to tell Starr?"

"I see no reason to say anything at all. Trey's dead."

"Hey, Jada, you take care of yourself."

"You too, Hunty!"

Jada was arguing on the phone with Shamari about her

not visiting him for the last couple of weeks when a text came through from Fresh. She told Shamari that she was going to get some rest and to call her back.

Fresh: *Can I come over?*

Jada: *My cycle started today.*

Fresh: *It's not all about sex with me.*

Jada: *Really? Could have fooled me.*

Fresh: *LMAO. You got jokes.*

Jada: *What you want with me, boy???*

Fresh: *Really? Are you on your cycle?????*

Jada: *Yes.*

Fresh: *Netflix and Chill. I wanna check this show called Narcos out. Everybody talking about it.*

Jada: *Don't tell me you ain't got Netflix. Netflix is only 7.99.*

Fresh: *I got it but I want to chill with you.*

Jada: *Netflix and Chill, huh? You better not touch me. I might let you rub my booty though.*

Fresh: *Text me that address. I'm going to put it in my GPS.*

Jada: *Okay.*

An hour later, Jada let Fresh in and they headed straight to the bedroom. She was wearing an oversized, light blue Under Armour sweatshirt and some wool PJs. She hopped right up on the bed and powered on the TV. He kicked his shoes off and dove into bed with her.

"I can't believe you came over."

"Why?"

"After I told you what I told you."

"Jada, you're my friend. I mean, I would have loved to hit that. But it ain't all about sex. I mean that ain't all I got on my mind."

"What else is on your mind?"

"Money."

"Mine too."

"I know."

"So where the food at?"

"You want me to order a pizza?"

"Yeah. You should have already done that. What do you think Netflix and Chill is?"

Netflix and Chill usually ends up with somebody's ass in

the air but it ain't gonna be my bloody ass tonight."
"You ever did it on your period?"
"Well kind of. Sorta."
"What you mean?"
She picked up her iPhone and dialed Papa John's. She ordered a medium thin crust with ground beef, pepperoni and mushrooms.
When she hung the phone up, he massaged her ass cheeks.
"Look, I don't do that."
"You just said you did."
"Well, it was this one guy I called Big Papa. He ate me out."
"That's disgusting."
"He was disgusting."
They laughed their asses off. They sat up in the bed and watched the show. Fifteen minutes later, the Papa John's guy came with the pizza. Jada sat the pizza in the bed between them.
Fresh folded a slice and stuffed it in his mouth.
Jada said, "So where is Q?"
"I guess at home. I don't know. I haven't talked to him today."
"Really?"
"You talk to Starr?"
"Not in a couple of days."
"She doing okay?"
"As far as I know."
"What made you ask about Q?"
"What kind of person is Q?"
"Smart and calculating."
"Manipulative?"
He laughed and said, "When I said calculating, I didn't mean it like that."
"Do you think he would hurt Starr? I mean physically harm her?"
"No. He loves her. Why?"
"Just asking."
"Kind of a strange question to be asking."
Jada sat her pizza down and said, "I want to ask you something, but I want you to promise not to tell Q."

"I promise."

"Did Q want Trey dead?"

"Who told you that?"

"I'm just asking."

"Someone must have told you that."

"Okay, someone told me."

"Who?"

"What difference does it make?"

Fresh said, "Look, you don't need to say shit about this to nobody. Trey is dead. This won't do nothing but cause more drama."

"Look, I'm not going to say anything. So it's true?"

Fresh didn't answer.

"It's true." Jada said.

"Don't mention this shit to Starr. You know how he feels about Starr." Fresh said.

"I wouldn't dare say shit about that."

She sat back down on the bed and there was a weird silence between them.

Then she said, "Look, I ain't saying shit, okay?"

Chapter 12

The sound of the gun cocking was all Black heard when he entered Fresh's home. Black turned and faced Fresh. The gun was aimed at the tip of his nose. Fresh was angry as hell.

"Why'd you do it, bruh?"

"Do what?"

"Talk to my plug behind my back. Don't play stupid, Black. He told me that you stopped and told him that you could help him move the weight."

Black hands were in the air in a pleading manner and he said, "You're right, man. I shouldn't have done that. Put that away before somebody gets hurt."

"Why in the hell did you do it, Black?"

"I had just got out of jail and I needed work."

So you see me eating with a Mexican, you assume it was the plug and you wanted to go around me?"

"I was wrong, man. Put the gun up, Fresh. Let's talk."

Fresh moseyed to the side of Black, the gun still pointed at Black. He had a direct shot at Black's noggin.

"Why should I let you live?"

Black looked at Fresh with pleading eyes. "Because it will not happen again."

Fresh lowered the gun. "That was foul, bruh."

"Look, I need work and I knew that you and Q wasn't going to fuck with me, but the dude who went with you to show you where Starr's nephew was my guy. I called one of my partnas to help us out."

"Black, I like you. I don't know why, but I like you."

"I'll never do it again."

"You better not." Fresh said. "The funny thing is that I had just made up my mind that I was going to do business with you."

"I appreciate it. You talk to Jada?"

"Last night. She doing okay."

"Hey, can we do some business now? I have a lawyer to pay. I need to make some extra bread."

"Yeah."

●   ●   ●

Terrell showed up at Starr's place of business unannounced. She said, "What are you doing here?"

"I came because you've been avoiding my calls."

"I haven't been avoiding nobody's calls."

"You haven't been answering my calls."

"I have been super busy."

"I haven't heard from you in three weeks."

"So you can shoot me a text."

All these questions were annoying her.

"Look, I was going to call you, all right?"

"So you like fucking dudes and cutting them off?"

"I'm sorry."

Terrell narrowed his eyes and clenched his teeth before frowning.

Starr swallowed hard. She knew Terrell didn't deserve to be treated the way she had treated him.

"Look, I understand you got a man."

"I don't have a man."

"Well then, what's the problem?"

"Look, I don't know what I want."

"I'm what you need."

"You think I don't know that?" She sighed and said, "It's not that simple."

"So you wanna keep dating D boys all your life?"

"You don't know shit about me!"

"Hey look, you're right. I don't know shit about you and you ain't trying to let me get to know you."

"Hey, I'm sorry. I shouldn't have yelled."

"It's okay," Terrell said.

"It's not okay. And I should have answered your calls or at least shot you a text back."

"What's wrong with me?"

"It's me." She avoided his eyes. "I guess I don't know what's best for me. I like shit to be complicated and I guess that's why I'm not married now."

"Do you regret sleeping with me?"

"I don't live with regrets."

"Was I good?"

"You were great, honey."

"Not great enough for you?"

She stared at the floor and clasped her hands. "No, but you are exactly what I need."

"Should I give up? Should I just say the hell with it?"

"No."

"You're so damn complicated."

"I know. I know. I'm crazy. Are you sure you want to deal with all that. Are you sure you can handle me?"

"I don't know, but I'll damn sure try."

"You will?" Her eyes lit up.

"You're worth the risk."

Chapter 13

Fresh lay in the bed with a stripper named Bambi when he heard a boom.

"Police! Come out with your hands up!"

Fresh turned to Bambi and said, "Be cool. I got this."

He stood from the bed and slid into a pair of sweatpants. He stepped into the living room and found six uniformed cops pointing Glock 22s inches away from his forehead.

F.B.I. Agent Daniels stepped forward. "On the floor, Mr. Mackins!"

There was a gun in the vent in the kitchen. Fresh knew that was automatic prison time for him if the police found it.

"Is there anyone else in here?"

The door opened and Bambi appeared, draped in a sheet. Her ass appeared shapely underneath the sheet.

"We want to search the place." Daniels said.

"For what?"

Daniels passed the search warrant to Fresh and he looked it over. They must have a confidential informant. He saw cocaine, automatic weapons and a large sum of cash listed on the warrant.

"This is bullshit." He crumpled the paper.

"If it's bullshit, then we'll be on our way. Save us the trouble of tearing up your house and show us where the dope is."

They ransacked Fresh's place. They cleaned out his kitchen cabinets, dumped the trashcans and searched through shoeboxes, pantries, his refrigerator, the bathroom toilets, sinks and mattresses. Fresh prayed that they didn't search the vent. Bambi munched on her fingernails.

"She's fine, bro." Daniels said.

"Creep," Bambi said. "Look, I don't live here, I just spent the night."

Fresh said, "Can you let her go?"

"We'll let her go when we're done with her."

Daniels powered on the television. "Do you mind if I watch ESPN?"

"Look, man, do what you're gonna do, so you can get the hell out of here."

They searched for fifteen more minutes and then a cop named Martinez said to Daniels, "Looks like there is nothing here."

Daniels said, "Search the vents and then we can go."

A white cop named Pressly came and said, "Boss, we hit the jackpot." He presented Daniels with a wad of cash, a 9mm and a 40 Cal.

Fresh said, "Fuck!"

"Fuck is right, playboy, because you're about to get fucked."

He cuffed Fresh who wanted to put a shirt on but they denied him that privilege. The girl was allowed to leave without arrest.

•   •   •

The sound of a horn honking startled Black. He glanced in his rear view mirror. Someone was waving for his attention. The F.B.I. agent. He pulled into the Publix parking lot and hopped out of the car. Daniels was sitting on the hood of his car.

"Dude, I can't be talking to you out here in public."

Daniels laughed. "Do I look like a cop?"

"But you are one." Black looked around. "What do you want?"

"You heard about what happened to your boy?"

"What boy?"

"Fresh."

"What happened to Fresh?"

"Oh we got him on some weapons charges. No big deal."

Black was stunned. He wondered how Daniels knew that he knew Fresh.

"I know everything."

"What happened?" Black crossed his arms. "What does this have to do with me?"

Daniels smiled. "It has everything to do with you." He lit a cigarette. "What's going to be really fucked up is when I describe the CI in the discovery motion."

"What?"

"The CI is a black man from Atlanta, that's been arrested multiple times for felony drug possession."

"What the fuck are you talking about?"

Daniels puffed his cigarette. "I'mma make it real simple. Either you help me or Fresh is going to think you set him up."

"Now why would he ever think that?"

"I saw you leaving his house the other day."

Black thought back to the day that he'd visited Fresh. The day that Fresh had drawn a gun on him.

"What?"

"You were the last male that visited his house."

"Fuck you."

"Look, man, I give you drugs and we all make money or I make it seem as though you set Fresh up. I let Homeland Security pick you up and nobody makes money."

"What do you want from me, bruh?"

"Let's be a team. Me and you. What is the hesitation, bruh? I'm just asking you to work with me. Protect yourself."

"How do I know I can trust you?"

"I'm from the hood just like you. The only difference between me and you is that you got caught."

"So you take shit from drug dealers and put it back on the street?"

"I save drug dealers."

"How is that?"

"Because when I take the shit, the evidence disappears and they get less time."

"I understand."

"I'll make Fresh's charges disappear.

"I work for you?"

"We'll be partners."

"You make my investigation go away?"

"Like 2014."

"I don't understand. You were working with the mayor?"

"I was. I was also in charge of his investigation."

"You tipped him that Sasha was trying to set him up?"

"I bugged her house. Playing both sides."

"So you told him what she did?"

"Maybe."

"But why did you let him walk in the trap in the first place?"

"He got greedy. He needed to be stopped. That's the only rule, Black. Don't ever get greedy."

"How will I know that?"

"I'll warn you."

"Greedy? He wasn't in the drug game?"

"Look, the way me and the mayor worked was he accepted bribes and he paid me to keep the heat off his ass. The situation he and I had had absolutely nothing to do with the drug game."

"So he wasn't charged?"

"I told him it's too hot for him. He's not in jail and he's not going to jail."

Black was trying to take all of this in as he stood analyzing this man that had been clearly following him and could make his life hell.

"Let me think about it."

"What is it to think about?"

"A lot."

"Don't make me go after that girlfriend. You know, the madam."

"I'll give you an answer in a few days."

"I'll even see if I can get Shamari out."

"Look, I'll be in touch."

Chapter 14

A crackhead named Sandy registered a room at the Hyatt in Lithonia in her name. After the room was secure, Brooke came over carrying a Victoria Secret's overnight bag. DeMontre was waiting for her. Brooke hugged him and dropped her bag at the foot of the bed. She sat in the recliner located in the corner of the room.

"What's wrong, shawty? It's not the end of the world."

She smiled "The end of my virginity."

He caressed her shoulders. "It's not so bad, shawty."

"Can you at least not call me shawty? Just for the day? I never imagined the man that was going to take my virginity was going to be calling me Shawty."

He toyed with her long, beautiful hair. "Anything for you, Brooke."

She smiled. "If we have sex, what does that mean?"

He lifted her tresses, kissed her neck and said, "It will mean that you're not a virgin anymore."

She turned and faced him, "That's not what I mean."

"You wanna know if I'm your boyfriend?" He laughed. "You have a boyfriend."

"We broke up."

"What you do that for?"

She stood from the bed and made a beeline for her bag. "This is a mistake. I can't do it."

"I've paid for this room, shawty."

"Would you quit calling me that?"

He stood in front of her and said, "Look, I've paid for this room."

"How much was the room?"

"A hundred and nineteen dollars."

She dug into her wallet and removed a hundred and twenty dollars. A red condom packet dropped on the floor.

He snagged it and said, "What's this?"

"You didn't think I was going to have unprotected sex did you? I'm seventeen. I ain't ready to be a parent."

"Me neither." He passed her the condom.

"Me either."

"Does it bother you when my grammar is not perfect?"

"No."

"Why do you correct me?"

"Habit."

He handed her the money back.

"Keep your money."

She sat back and he sat on the bed and she said, "What do you like about me?"

"I dunno. I guess you represent something that I ain't. Something that I wish I could be. You feel me?"

"What's stopping you from becoming what you wish you could be?"

"I ain't get all the opportunities like you."

"You're seventeen. Just like me."

He lit a cigarette.

"I didn't know you smoked."

"I'm not a real smoker I might smoke three cigarettes a week."

"Cigarettes are a gateway drug to—"

"I don't need the preaching."

"So what are we going to do?"

"You're the girl. Nothing happens unless you say so."

"I can't just give my goodies up to anybody. I wish you was

my boyfriend, but since you're not."

"You wish I were your boyfriend, you mean."

She laughed. "See, you do have good grammar."

"I guess so. I'm not mad though. You want to cuddle?"

"You going to report it back to your brother and 'em?"

"Fuck them." He put the cigarette out and hopped under the cover. She peeled out of her jeans and revealing a G-String. She got in the bed and pushed her ass against his rock hard dick and he said, "What a time to be alive."

"Drake?"

"No. Dat ass."

They laughed their asses off.

• • •

TeTe invited Black to her house. Eli and Butterfly greeted him at the door. They had been playing. Butterfly hugged Black.

"Do you have any money?" she asked.

Black removed his wallet and gave her a hundred dollars.

Butterfly smiled and said, "Don't tell Mommy I asked."

"I won't. What are you going to do with it?"

"Save it. I don't spend my own money, but I like to have it."

"Smart girl."

She disappeared into her bedroom. And when the door closed, Eli said, "So, Black, what exactly are your intentions here?"

Black sized up Eli. He was an inch taller than Black but buffed. Black knew he could whip his ass and if he couldn't, he would shoot his ass.

"So what made you start coming around? Where did you come from?"

"Where the fuck did you come from? Let me clarify one thing, bruh. I got my own money. I don't need no bitch to take care of me."

"I didn't say you did."

"You got something against me?"

"No. Looks like she loves you. I'm just trying to make sure that you love her. TeTe is my best friend."

"Best friends cut fingers off?"

"That's the past."

"Just like your relationship with her."

TeTe gazed down from the top of the stairway then signaled for Black to come up. When Black moseyed up the stairs, she said, "I've been waiting on you."

"For what?"

"I want to fuck."

"He's here."

She smiled and placed his hand on her ass. "I don't give a damn about him. He wanted to see Butterfly."

She stripped. "I want you inside of me."

"He will hear us."

"And that will turn me on."

He peeled out of his clothes and she plopped on her knees. She removed his dick from his shorts and slurped it. He reclined on the bed and she straddled. She felt him inside her ribcage.

"Oh my God! Black, you feel so good."

"I can't believe we're doing this."

"This is my fucking house. I'll do what I want. Do you care about his feelings?"

"I don't.

"And neither do I. Now shut up and fuck me."

Chapter 15

Q STROKED STARR'S HAIR AS SHE LAY ON HIS BARE chest.

"I gotta pee." Q said.

Starr inched away from his chest. She watched his ass as he dashed to the bathroom. He returned moments later and took his position. They faced each other. Both of them were smiling hard. He inched close to her and tried to steal a kiss.

He made a sad face. "What's wrong?"

"My breath is all stinky."

"You're kidding me, right?"

"No."

"What? Give me a kiss, woman."

He approached her and she blinked. He kissed her on the lips.

"You satisfied?" she asked.

"I want some tongue."

"That's nasty."

"If we're going to be together, we have to be able to deal with each other's bad breath, farts and all."

"I don't want to think about farts. Boys always want to think about farts."

"Oh, you don't fart?"

"I do! Could you quit talking about that? That's nasty."

He laughed. "I guess you're right. So are we going to be together?" Q asked.

"I never said that."

"You are right here where you want to be."

She smiled. "I am."

"Otherwise, you wouldn't be here."

"You're right."

"I know I'm right. That basketball player ain't got shit on me."

Her mind shifted to Terrell. She wondered how he was doing for a moment. She actually felt bad for him.

"What are you thinking about?"

"Huh?"

"I said something about the basketball player and your mind drifted."

"I was thinking about T.J."

"Where is he?"

"He's at Trey's mom's house."

"How has he been?"

"He's been good. Trying to convince me to let him play tackle football because there are two other boys in his classes playing."

"So why won't you?"

"My dad said to let him play flag."

"Flag is for sissies."

"My daddy was a football star in high school. He says that T.J.'s brain is still developing and he can play tackle when he is eleven or twelve."

"Okay, I can dig that."

There was an awkward silence and then he said, "I wanna ask you a question?"

"What?"

"Did you fuck the football player?"

"You mean the basketball player?"

He laughed and said, "We were talking about T.J. playing football. It kind of messed me up, but you know what I meant."

They both stared at each other and neither would break their glance.

"Did you?"

"And if I did?"

"I guess I would have to live with it."

"Why are you asking me this?"

"Because you asked me if I slept with Chanel."

"And you lied like you did."

"I know. I hope she never finds out."

"You lied to me. How is she gonna find out?"

"Starr did you sleep with him or not?"

"I did."

His eyes protruded. "What?"

"Look, I'm sorry I slept with him. I was vulnerable. I thought you had slept with Chanel and I was lonely and he was nice, so I slept with him."

He rose from the bed and slid into his pajama pants. He grabbed a tank top from the dresser and said, "I can't believe you."

She sat up on the bed. She tried to read his mind. He looked disgusted with her, like she was a ten-dollar whore on the corner. But she knew how men were. Even if he had slept with Chanel, he still would have been pissed.

She stood from the bed and grabbed a pair of Victoria Secrets shorts that were lying on the floor near the bed. She put them on as he disappeared into his walk-in closet.

He came back with her overnight bag and said, "You should go."

"I should go where, motherfucker?"

"You should leave, Starr."

"Okay, so it's okay for you to ride around fucking with other bitches, and the minute I do what you are doing, you get pissed?"

"I never slept with that woman."

"I didn't know that."

"So you wanted to get back at me?"

"Look, I was lonely. I told you that."

She tried to embrace him but he slipped away from her grip.

"Leave, Starr."

"I ain't leaving."

"Cool. I'm leaving."

"And I'll be here when you come back."

He removed his pajama pants and slid into a pair of jeans and a Polo shirt and then walked right past her.

She plopped to the floor and cried.

Chapter 16

IT WAS THURSDAY NIGHT AT MOE'S AND JOE'S AND THE drinks were on special. Jada and Starr sipped Mojitos. Jada liked the place. Even though she could usually find some poor sucker to buy her drinks, she liked the cheap drinks. This way she didn't have to entertain somebody all night that spent a few coins on drinks.

"So what's on your mind?"

"So much."

Jada shook her head then flagged the waitress who ran over. "Hey, this one is kinda weak. Where is the liquor?"

"I'll take it back to the bartender."

"Yes, because this is Kool-Aid."

"You were saying?"

"I've been really missing Lani this week."

"I've been thinking about her too."

"Really?"

"Every time it rains. I still have my phobia about windshield wipers. They were the last sound I heard when I was on the other end of the phone. Listening to her get murdered."

"Damn."

"I think I'm going to go to therapy about it."

"I think you should." Starr said.

The waitress delivered the drink.

Jada tasted it. "This is much better, honey."

When she was gone, Starr said, "Have you ever fucked somebody that you regretted fucking?"

"No. If I fucked you, it's because I wanted to fuck you."

Starr laughed at her bluntness, but she knew that Jada was being truthful.

"What's wrong?"

"There is this guy I met. He is a client of mine. Played in the NBA. He likes me and long story short, I thought Q had screwed this Chanel girl, so I fucked him. Then I admitted to Q that we had slept together."

"You did what?"

"I know. I should have taken it to my grave."

"I know."

"So what makes you think he didn't sleep with this Chanel girl? You believe him?"

"I do."

"I don't."

"'Why?"

"I don't trust niggas."

Starr laughed.

"No, seriously. I'm dealing with this dude now that's damn near married."

Starr didn't like hearing about Jada's excursions with men that were taken.

"Q tried to put me out of his place last night."

"Tried?"

"I didn't leave."

Starr gulped her drink down.

A country-ass dude in a red three-piece suit who sat two tables over waved his hands, trying to get Jada's attention. She noticed him but ignored him.

The waitress appeared and said, "That guy wants to buy the next round of drinks."

Jada made eye contact with the man then blew a kiss his way. "Thanks, baby, but I can handle this myself."

The cornball yelled. "Both of y'all fine as hell." He

embarrassed them. The tacky red suit made him look as if he was straight from the peach orchards of Georgia.

Starr mocked him, "Both of y'all fine as hell."

They both laughed their asses off. The waitress dropped more drinks off.

Starr said, "So what do I do to get him back?"

Jada asked the waitress to see the menu, but she really wasn't hungry. Paying attention to the menu would give her time to think of something to tell Starr.

She was the one that had wanted to take a break from her relationship. Then she had gone and fucked another man—a man that she clearly didn't want. She would have passed judgment but she had been there before. Starr was clearly dick-dumb right now.

"So you're going to tell me how I should go about getting him back?"

"Do you want him back?"

"I do."

"Do you really want him or do you want him because he don't want you?"

"I don't know what I want."

"I can't help you on this one, sis."

"I'm just glad you are here to listen to me."

"No problem. I have a question to ask you."

"What?"

"How much do you really know about Q? I mean, I know you know that he was Trey's plug but what else do you know about him? I don't know a lot about him, but do you really know him? I think if you do get back with him, you should really get to know him. Try to meet his kids. His mama. See what his baby mamas have to say about him."

Starr said, "Have you gotten to know Fresh?"

"I don't need to get to know him. Fresh ain't serious."

"When was the last time you seen him."

"Came over the other day for Netflix and chill action."

"Did that chill end up with your ass in the air?"

"Nope, but it could have been if I wasn't on my cycle. I ain't going to lie. I would have fucked him for sure."

They both laughed.

The waitress brought more drinks.

"Yeah, baby girl, just get to know him better."

"Wait, have you heard something about him?"

"No." Jada said as she thought back to the day at the mall when she ran into Shantelle.

"Are you sure?"

"I am."

"If you heard something, would you tell me?"

"Absolutely."

Starr said, "I love you Jada."

"Let's take an Usie."

"You going to post it on Instagram?"

"You know it."

Jada took a picture of her and Starr smiling and posted it on Instagram with the captioned: *Date night/w Bae.*

•   •   •

It was nine p.m. when Fresh and Black met at the Waffle House on Piedmont.

After they were seated, Fresh said, "Feds raided my house and took me to jail."

"What?" Black sounded surprised. although he knew that he'd been locked up.

"What happened?"

"They came with some bogus warrant talking about a CI told them that they'd seen me with drugs, money, and weapons. I need a good attorney."

"Joey Turch. He's the best in Atlanta."

"Joey Turch, huh?"

Black scrolled to Joey's number and dialed his number.

"Tyrann, I was just thinking about calling you."

"Oh, really?"

"I'm going to file for dismissal of your charges. The state doesn't have anyone to testify."

"Great."

"Hey, I'm in the middle of dinner. Can I call you back?"

"Need to ask you something."

"Make it quick."

"I have a friend from Houston. Feds raided his house."

"You know I'm not cheap."

"Money's not a problem."

"What's his name? I'll look over the case when I get a chance."

"His name is Desmond Mackins. I need you to make this go away."

"I'll look into it."

Chapter 17

DANIELS WAS WEARING A BLUE NYLON JACKET WITH THE letters F.B.I. stitched on it in gold letters. Black realized that he really was the F.B.I. Black was meeting Daniels at an office business park outside in Barrow County. At the back entrance was a warehouse dock. The dock door was open and Daniels and Black stood and talked on the dock.

Daniels was rocking back and forth from leg to leg and Black supposed that he must have been nervous. But he could not have been as nervous as Black was. Black was sure that any given moment, the police were going to jump out and arrest him.

Daniels passed Black a bag and said, "There is ten kilos in here. I need three hundred thousand dollars."

"I don't have the money."

"You better have it in a week."

"You're asking a lot."

"I'm giving a lot.

"And if I don't?"

"You will." Daniels lit a cigarette and said, "There's more—when you're done."

"You got any heroin?"

"That kills people."

"And coke doesn't?"

"My sister OD'd off it, so I have my reasons."

"I see."

"What about my friend's charges?"

"It's going to get tossed. I spoke to Joey Turch. He asked me to do him a favor. He's going to file a motion to suppress. I'm going to give him information to get it suppressed."

"But you said you were going to get it dismissed anyway."

Daniels smiled and puffed on the cigarette. "Look, I'm just playing the game."

"You're playing to win."

"Don't we all wanna win?" Daniels thumped the cigarette out in front of the dock.

"You're a shrewd guy."

"You can call me that."

"I need to ask one more question about the mayor."

"Why do you give a damn about the mayor?"

"Because he was working with you and he still went down. You were investigating him and you was protecting him at the same time."

"He was greedy. And I don't want to talk about that anymore. Meet me right here in exactly one week at the same time with the money and I'll have more for you."

Black hopped off the dock and climbed into the car.

Daniels said, "If you need any favors let me know."

"I have my own brand of justice."

•   •   •

Starr lay on the floor in the bathroom that connected to her office. She clenched onto the toilet seat. She held on and vomited. It was the third time that day. She didn't want to work, but she had to. There was nobody to replace her. She would go in for a few hours. Brooke arrived at two thirty and Starr instructed Brooke to take over for the rest of the day. Before she left, she called her mother and told her what was going on with her.

"You ain't pregnant are you?" her mother asked.

"What? No!"

"How do you know?"

"I'm not."

"Take the test. Sounds like a bun in the oven."

"I don't believe I'm pregnant."

"Why?"

"I don't know. I just don't feel like I'm pregnant."

"Take the test."

On the way home, Starr stopped and purchased a home pregnancy test from CVS. As soon as she got home, she disappeared into the bathroom. She smiled when she saw the double lines, but she was not happy about the circumstances. She telephoned Jada, who came over right away.

"What was so urgent that you wanted me to come over here right away?"

Starr's eyes averted to the pregnancy stick that was on the table.

Jada picked it up and said, "Congratulations, boo."

Starr was looking really sad and Jada said, "What's wrong?"

"Look, I want a baby, but I didn't want it to be like this. Not at my age. I'm too old not to be married."

"Hey, that's the way it goes sometimes."

"Have you told Q?"

"He's still not speaking to me."

"You have to talk to him."

"I know." Tears welled up in Starr's eyes. Jada took a seat behind her and massaged her shoulders.

"It's going to be alright. Are you going to keep it?"

"I don't know. What would you do?"

"That's a tough one. You know I ain't the baby type. I'll be an auntie, but I don't know if I'll ever be ready to be a mommy."

Starr sighed and said, "I want a daughter since I have T.J."

"You can name her Lani."

"What a good idea."

"You have to tell Q."

She dialed his number and the voicemail picked up.

Q received a call saying that Diego was in the lobby waiting to see him. This time Q invited him up. Outside on the balcony, they smoked cigars and stared off into the Atlanta skyline.

"Look, I need you."

Q puffed his cigar and said, "I need you to quit telling people that I wanted Trey murdered."

"You realize I never met Trey?"

Q coughed and said, "I know."

"So why are you here?"

"I know you want me dead."

Q didn't respond. Of course he wanted Diego dead.

"Can I offer you a million dollars? To make amends for what I did?

"You can give it to Rico's family."

Q said, "You're working with Fresh. What do you want with me?"

"Fresh is not you. He's young. He likes to party." Diego paused, then stared out into the Atlanta night, then he turned and faced Q. "Me and you, we're businessmen. Gentlemen."

"Are you serious?" Q laughed. "You consider yourself a gentleman?"

"Just as much a gentleman as you are."

"What is that supposed to mean?"

"You and I know that for whatever reason you had, you wanted Trey dead. A man that you had told me was one of your best friends."

Q turned his back on Diego.

Diego grabbed Q's shoulder, "Look, I don't judge you, my friend."

Q faced him again. "Don't touch me."

"Listen to me, Q."

"I'm listening."

"So what do you want me to do, Q? Do you want me to tell Fresh that I made the whole thing up about Trey? If you want, I can tell him I was lying."

"But you wasn't lying."

"I want to give you what I owe you."

"What's stopping you from doing that?"

"Will you work with me? My uncle is going to give me a big shipment and I need your help."

"Can you give me a thousand today?"

"Tonight."

"This is between you and I. Fresh doesn't need to know this." Q said.

"I won't tell him."

"And don't give him any more product. He needs to get it from me."

"Are you going to keep working with Gordo?"

"How did you know I was working with him?"

"He's my cousin."

"Gordo and I have an understanding."

"You realize me and Gordo have the same product?"

"I know."

"And you're going to get rid of mine and his?"

"With a few phone calls."

"That's why you are so valuable."

"I know."

"I don't know why you ever wanted to get out of the business in the first place."

"I thought I could go straight."

Diego laughed.

Chapter 18

FRESH SLAMMED HIS CAR IN REVERSE. HE BARRELED out of the parking lot of the Forum Athletic Club. He'd had an amazing chest and ab workout with a trainer. When he had finished, he had received a text from Jada.

Jada: *Netflix and Chill?*

Fresh: *When?*

Jada: *Duh...Now!!!!*

Fresh: *Period????*

Jada: *Lol. No.*

Fresh: *Leaving the gym. Let me go home and change clothes.*

Jada: *Perfect.*

Two hours later, Fresh arrived at Jada's house and they headed straight to the bedroom. Jada put on Narcos. She was wearing some green booty shorts that were fighting hard to contain her voluptuous ass.

Fresh slapped her on the ass and she said, "Boy, if you don't stop..."

"What?"

"Let's watch Narcos first."

Fresh removed his Jordan's and hoped into her bed.

Jada said, "You need to take those jeans off if you're going to be in my bed."

He laughed and removed his jeans. Fresh rested in her bed wearing only his pinstriped boxer briefs. She was turned on by the impression of his dick, even though Mr. Tank had put on quite the show himself.

"So, what's up with Starr?"Fresh asked.

"Seen her the other day."

"Did you tell her what you knew?"

Jada looked perplexed. "About what I know?"

"You know, about what you found out about Q and Trey?"

"No. I told you I wasn't going to say shit. You didn't believe me?"

"I did."

"Well, why did you ask me?"

"I dunno. I know you and Starr are pretty close."

"You didn't believe me. You just sayin' that you didn't believe me."

He laughed and said, "I didn't believe you."

"Look, they have enough problems without me adding one more."

"What's wrong?"

"I'm sure Q will tell you when the time comes."

"What the hell is that supposed to mean?"

"Now, I need to know if you can keep your mouth shut."

He said, "I cross my heart and hope to die." And with his index finger he made a crossing motion.

"You're so damn silly," she said.

"What is it?"

"Starr is pregnant."

"No!"

"Yes."

"Q didn't tell me."

"They ain't speaking right now. She hasn't told him. He won't answer the phone."

"Damn. Is she gonna keep it?"

"That's a decision that they are going to have to make."

"And what about the decision that we are going to have to make?"

"What decision is that?"

He placed his hands on her thigh and said, "At what point are those panties coming down. Q and Starr's kid need a playmate."

She slid her hips up and removed her shorts and panties.

Chapter 19

BLACK LAY ON THE SOFA WITH HIS MOUTH OPEN. HIS
faced pressed against a spit-drenched pillow. A fly
crawled on his ear and he swatted at it unsuccessfully.
His cell phone rang and it startled him. He turned his
head in the direction of the phone lying on the floor and
that's when the fly entered his mouth. He swallowed it
before he could spit it out.

The phone was still ringing and his arm fished for the
phone that was lying underneath the sofa. It stopped
ringing before he could pick it up. He'd missed a call from
Bird. A minute later, he received another call from Bird.

"Black, you forgot about me?"

"No. I ain't forgot. I had some things I needed to take care
of."

"I have Avant, but I need you to hand over the bread."

"I'm going to need a couple of days in order to come up
with that kind of money."

"Come on, Black. I know you got the money. Word on the
street is that you're loaded."

"Sounds like extortion."

"I wouldn't call it extorting. It's my way of letting you

know something has to be done about the loss."

"I'm going to need a couple of days."

"That tab needs to be paid."

"So, you think that you are going to come into my city and tell me what the fuck to do? It don't work like that."

"Look, homie. I know I ain't from around here but you must not know how far the Crips can reach. I can have you touched. Even if you go to jail, I can have you fucked up. Look, give me what I ask for and I will give you what you need."

"Give me a few days."

• • •

Sapphire primped in front of the mirror. Her lashes looked dazzling. Her teeth freshly whitened. She loved her smile right now. Tonight, she would debut her turquoise blue hair. It was almost rent time and she needed to make at least fifteen hundred dollars tonight.

The doorbell rang. She wasn't expecting company. She walked up to the peephole. It was her co-worker Champagne.

She opened the door. "Girl, what are you doing here?"

"I need to talk to you."

Sapphire invited her in when suddenly Black wedged his foot in the door before it closed.

Sapphire screamed, "Oh my God!"

Black waved a silver Glock 40 and said, "One more sound and yo ass is dead."

TeTe marched inside and said to Champagne, "Get the fuck out of here. Wait outside and make sure nobody comes in here."

TeTe scanned her house. She was kind of impressed with the stripper's taste. TeTe studied the woman's face before saying, "Don't I know you?"

Sapphire didn't answer and Black slapped the fuck out of her. "Did you hear her ask you a question?"

"Yes."

"Where do I know you from?" TeTe asked again.

"I met you through Todd. He was trying to recruit me to

work for your ho house."

"My escort service, you mean?"

TeTe approached her and grabbed a handful of ass and kissed her on the neck. "Why didn't I hire you?"

"My weight."

TeTe slapped her on the ass and said, "Well, it looks like you've been fucking. Were you too skinny?"

"No, you said I was too thick. Said that you had mostly white and foreign clients."

"Oh yeah, I remember now. He brought you to my suite at the Ritz."

"Exactly."

"You're gorgeous."

"Thank you."

TeTe said to Black, "Let's have a ménage."

Black grinned. "Now?"

"Why not now?" TeTe said.

Sapphire removed her phone from her purse trying to unlock her screen without looking at it. If she could do that, she could dial 911.

TeTe knocked the phone from her hand and it crashed on the floor shattering the screen. TeTe scooped it up and handed it back to her.

"Don't you hate when that happens? Did you know Todd was dead?" TeTe asked.

"He's dead?"

"Just like Cato."

"Cato? Who is Cato?"

"My friend that Todd murdered," Black said.

"I can explain."

"Please."

"I—"

TeTe stopped Sapphire by putting her lips on Sapphire's mouth. She tasted Sapphire's lips and put her hands around Sapphire's tiny waist then her hand traveled down the small of her back before cupping her ass.

"Stop."

"Oh baby! We are just starting."

TeTe removed her pink .380 from her purse and aimed it

at Sapphire's temple. "Now, you wanna tell me about the Detroit boys?"

"What do you want to know?"

"Full names and addresses."

"I don't know their address. But their names are Jabril and Rakeem Campbell."

"How do you know that?"

"I used to mess around with Jabril."

"You used to fuck the man, you mean?"

"Yes."

"And you don't know where he lives?"

"No."

"You really are a dumb ho.Give Black some head."

"What?"

Black removed his dick from his pants and TeTe lower the gun. She stuffed it back in her purse and stripped. Sapphire took Black deep inside her mouth. Black ran his finger through her hair. He relished the warmth of her mouth. She was good at what she did, but every so often, he felt her teeth.

TeTe licked Sapphire's clit as she fondled herself at the same time. Sapphire moaned. Black flipped her over. Her ass was now facing him and her mouth was inches away from TeTe's kitty.

TeTe forced Sapphire's head between TeTe's legs. TeTe's hands fingered Sapphire's hair and she fucked Sapphire's mouth as Black entered Sapphire.

Black stepped back and TeTe kissed Sapphire. "You're so sexy."

"Thank you."

"I love your lips."

"Thanks."

She turned to Black and said, "Give me my purse."

Black passed her the purse and TeTe removed a pink strap-on. She fastened the toy around her waist and entered Sapphire's wet kitty.

Black couldn't believe his luck. He nursed his dick, trying his best to get it erect.

TeTe laughed and said, "Damn, you have two gorgeous women and you can't get yourself up?"

Black continued to stroke.

TeTe said, "Just put it in her mouth."

Seconds later, he inserted it in Sapphire's mouth and Black's head tilted back. "This feels amazing," he said. His eyes were still shut.

And when it was evident that Black was enjoying himself a bit too much, TeTe removed the gun from her purse and fired a shot that ripped into Sapphire's spine. When Sapphire keeled over, TeTe fired another bullet into the back of Sapphire's head.

Black was scrambling and trying to pull his underwear up at the same time. His eyes on TeTe. The pink strap-on was still around her waist.

She was laughing and said, "You was enjoying that shit too much."

"You're crazy."

She aimed the gun at him. Black shielded his face with his hands.

She lowered the gun and tossed it in her purse. "No worries, babe. You live to see another day."

"So damn crazy."

"That's what you like."

Black looked at Sapphire, who was lying there lifeless and said, "We have a body on our hands."

"We do." TeTe smiled, putting the strap-on back in her purse.

"You can't keep that on you. You have her DNA on it."

"We get her key from her. I'll call my friend John over and he'll come and clean the scene. He's a private investigator."

Black shook his head and said, "You have it all figured out, don't you?"

"I do."

"What about the witness?"

Champagne waited outside. TeTe called her inside. She came inside and saw Sapphire's dead body on the floor. TeTe pointed the gun at her but before TeTe could fire, Black tackled TeTe.

"What the fuck are you doing, Black?" She struggled with him.

He said, "You can't kill her."

Champagne fell to her knees and said, "Please, don't kill me. I'll do anything you want me to do. Just don't kill me. I haven't seen shit. I promise I won't tell anyone."

"I don't believe her."

Black approached TeTe with pleading eyes. "She helped us. We can't kill everybody. She is my friend."

"Look, this can come back on us." TeTe lowered the gun.

Black started getting dressed.

"I'll call my friend John. He'll clean up and get rid of the body."

"Did he get rid of Todd's body?"

"Yes."

"Where?"

"For me to know and you to find out."

TeTe made her way over to Sapphire's dead body and squeezed her ass again. "Damn, what a shame. She had such an incredible body."

"She did."

"You owe me one."

"What?"

"A threesome."

"I never thought you like girls."

"When I see one I like." She winked at him.

Chapter 20

GORDO WAS SIPPING AN ICED MOCHA FROM STARBUCKS'S
when he showed up at Q's penthouse.

Q handed him two suitcases full of money, then said, "I spoke to Diego."

"Does Fresh know?" Gordo asked.

"No."

"Good. I don't want anyone to know, especially not my uncle. If he finds out, I'm a dead man."

"Nobody is going to find out unless your guys fuck it up."

"It's going to be a clean hit. I promise you. Nobody is going to get hurt except Diego."

Q studied Gordo's face. He couldn't believe that Gordo was going to murder his own cousin—a blood relative. But he knew that Gordo felt really bad for Rico's death and there was the fact that Diego had set his operation up right here in Atlanta and had become the competition. Gordo knew there was lots of money to be made in Atlanta, but the only way to get that money was for Diego to die.

"When are they going to do the job?"

"In two weeks."

"Who are they?"

"The less you know the better."

"Mexican?"

"Yes."

"Good."

"Do you want his head?"

"No. What the hell am I going to do with his head?"

Gordo laughed and said, "I thought you would want to see that the job was done."

Q couldn't believe that Gordo was talking about killing his own cousin so easy. But he knew that where Gordo and Diego were from, life didn't mean shit. The only thing that mattered was having mucho dinero.

"Take a picture."

"So is all the money here?" Gordo pointed to the suitcases.

"Everything."

"I love you, manu," Gordo said.

"I love you too, brother."

"Let's take over the world."

"Let's do it."

Gordo laughed and said, "Until you want to retire."

"I don't want to retire."

"What changed your mind?"

"I thought I was ready to settle down."

"With one woman?"

Q laughed. "Of course."

"Why would you do something like that? What the hell was you thinking, manu?"

"I wasn't thinking. I was pussy whipped."

"Pussy whipped? What is that?"

Q had forgotten that he had to be careful when speaking to Gordo. Although he understood most English words, he didn't understand slang.

"It's like when you cannot think; you have pussy on your brain."

Gordo laughed and said, "Oh...pussy whipped."

He sounded delighted that he'd learned a new term. He gulped down the coffee and picked up the suitcases.

It was eight p.m. when Fresh called Q and suggested that they meet at the Cigar City Club and at nine fifteen they met. They sat in the back on a burgundy leather sofa and they both toked on premium cigars.

Fresh inhaled and said, "Have you spoken to Starr?"

"No."

"Why?" Fresh asked.

"I don't want to talk about it."

"Look, I think you better talk to her."

"What do you know?"

"I don't know shit."" Fresh tried to lie and Q kept pressing.

"Look, Jada made me promise not to say nothing, so when you finally talk to Starr, you didn't hear this shit from me."

"What?"

"Starr's pregnant."

"What?"

"No wonder she has been blowing me up. I wonder why she just didn't text me and let me know that."

"I don't know. Maybe she wanted to have the conversation in person. Pregnancy is a pretty big deal, you know?"

"I don't need no more kids."

"I thought you wanted more?"

"I don't need another baby mama."

"I thought Starr was the one. She was the one that you were trying to leave the game for."

"She ain't the one."

"What happened, bruh?"

"I don't want to talk about it right now. Seriously."

"Okay, but you need to call Starr."

"I will."

Chapter 21

STARR WAS VENTING TO JADA NEEDED SOMEONE TO TALK to because ever since she found out that she was pregnant, she hadn't been able to get any rest. She's been stressed, although technically, T.J. had already made her a single mom. She was ashamed to tell her family that she was pregnant and not married. Even though she was sure they would be happy for her.

She remembered how upset her father was when Meeka was pregnant. Meeka was a child at the time when she got pregnant. They would be disappointed too. Only because she wasn't married.

"I don't know if I want to be a Mom."

"Why not?"

"I'm afraid."

"Afraid of what? You're already a mom."

"I know, but this is different."

Jada ate some nachos and said, "What's different?"

"Me and Q ain't in a good space and I don't wanna be alone on this."

"You're not alone. I'm here. You have a wonderful family and I was just at Lani's mom's house the other day. She was like, I wish you or Starr would hurry up and have a baby so I can be a grandma."

Starr smiled. "Did she really say that?"

"She sure did."

Starr sighed. "I don't know, Jada." She picked up a handful of nachos then said, "You didn't tell anyone I was pregnant, did you?"

"No." Jada lied. Now she regretted like hell telling Fresh. She would have to call him and make sure to remind him to keep his goddamned mouth shut.

"Good. I really don't want to have an abortion."

"I understand. Look, you should think about it first before you rush and do something crazy. And you should let him know. Even if you don't want to keep the baby."

"I don't want to tell him. He's acting like an asshole, Jada. I'm afraid this is the real Q. This is just how he is."

"He has a right to know."

"I don't want to tell him."

"You have to."

Starr and Jada made eye contact and Starr said, "Jada, whatever you do, just don't tell anyone my secret."

"I'll never tell anyone."

$$\bullet \quad \bullet \quad \bullet$$

John, TeTe's private investigator, sat alone at a table at Starbuck's in Buckhead stirring a latte and working on a word puzzle. TeTe approached and sat across from him. She removed her jacket and placed it on the back of the chair.

"Look, I need a favor."TeTe said.

"What is it?"

"I murdered someone and I need you to clean it up."

John scanned the Starbuck's and then he placed his hands over his lips and said, "Shhh. You never know who might be listening."

"Look, can you help me or not?"

"I can." John sipped his coffee and his glasses slid down the tip of his nose. "And I will."

"Okay, I need a couple of favors."

"I imagine that you want me to go and clean up the crime scene first. Where is the body?"

TeTe passed John a piece of paper containing Sapphire's address. "You need you go there right away. Before the body starts smelling."

"What's the other thing you need?"

"I need you to find someone."

"Who?"

"A couple of dudes that have been making threats. They want to kill me and my daughter. So I have to get them before they get me."

John sipped his coffee.

"You wanna kill them?"

"Yes. I want to end their lives."

"You say that so casually."

"You know how I am, John. Stop the bullshit."

"So these guys that you want dead, what are their names?"

"Rakeem and Jabril Campbell. Their brother was named Shakur. He got murdered a few months ago."

"Okay."

"And I have something for you."

John smiled. He knew what that meant. Whenever he did favors for her, he knew that she would have some young pussy waiting for him.

TeTe showed him the picture of a young Filipino girl named Banta. She had long hair, a nice ass and a chest like a twelve-year-old boy. John liked them like that. Although he would never have sex with anyone under eighteen, he loved them barely legal.

John's smile was perverted.

TeTe was disgusted by him, but she needed his old ass.

John said, "You got any girls with braces?"

"What?" TeTe's lips curled and she refused to look at him.

"I have a braces fetish."

"This is not middle school."

"I've always liked braces."

"There is one girl that wears a retainer."

"How old is she."

"She's twenty-four."

"Way too old."

"Look, I need you to find these guys before it's too fucking late. You understand me?"

"I understand. I'm going to need three thousand."

"Three thousand to find someone?"

"Let me remind you that you have a dead body on your hands."

"I'll get you the money."

TeTe stood and hugged John.

She stormed out and ordinarily she would be self-conscious about what she was wearing, but she knew that John didn't want her old, old ass.

• • •

Fy-head stood up from the booth twerking in hot pink yoga pants showing off her new ass implants to Miss America. An elderly white couple in the booth parallel to their table turned their noses up and then flagged the waiter. They asked to be moved across the room. As the waitress ushered the old white couple away, the old woman eyed Fy-head.

Fy-head said, "Go on wit yo' old ass. Don't nobody care if you move!"

Miss America said, "Girl, you a mess."

"Fuck her."

"I must admit, he did a nice job on your ass."

"You like it?"

"Yas! Bitch."

"You should get him to do yours."

"Look, he's mad as hell at me. He knows that I know where you at but he can't prove it. He threatened me but crazy-ass TeTe showed up and glued his hands to his balls."

"That's what she told me. I wasn't there, but she told me that she found him and glued his hands to his balls and told him to keep his hands to himself."

The bartender waiter came back and they ordered pina coladas. Five minutes later, the drinks were delivered.

"I ain't worrying 'bout that white man."

"I know you ain't worried about him, but I am. He knows me

and when I came home the other day, one of my neighbors told me that a white man was looking for me."

"You think it was him?"

"I know it was him."

"How do you know?"

"The way they described him."

"Yeah, it probably was his bitch ass. I was talking to my ex, Bobby, and he told me that he'd come by there looking for me. Bobby pulled a knife out and robbed his ass."

"What?"

"Bobby said he was over there with the police pointing out the house and all."

"No way!"

"I'm telling you."

"So I guess y'all spent all the money?"

"That money is long gone."

"Just great. Now I gotta dodge this motherfucker while you go on living your life."

"I'll call him."

"And tell him what? You know that man wants his money back."

"I'll call him and tell him that J-Will fucked me out of the money and beat my ass and I was just too afraid to tell him. And then I will give him J-Will's number."

"J-Will will flip on your ass for real."

"J-Will ain't worried about dat cracker."

They both laughed their asses off.

But then Miss America got serious. "I'm afraid. Look this man is pissed and he keeps bothering me."

"Next time he calls you. Meet up with him and call me. I'll get J-Will and we'll come to your room and drag his ass out and take him to Florida. We'll dump him in a lake and let the gators eat his ass."

Miss America laughed. Fy-head sipped her drink and said, "I'm serious. We kill him."

Chapter 22

Q PHONED STARR BUT DIDN'T GET AN ANSWER. HE WENT into her place of business and Brooke informed him that she wasn't there. He called her father but he hadn't heard from her. He then high-tailed it to her building, but she refused to let him come to her home. He decided to pay Jada a visit. When Q sat down, he crossed his legs, and this annoyed the hell out of Jada. Men that crossed their legs were so feminine. She avoided looking in his direction.

"Starr is pregnant." Q said.

Jada said, "Is she?" She sounded surprised.

Fresh had run his mouth, but this didn't surprise her considering Q was sitting in the living room with his legs crossed like a bitch.

"Come on, Jada. That's your best friend."

"She is."

"So you mean to tell me that she didn't tell you she was pregnant?"

"She ain't tell me shit."

"Call her."

"I tried."

"Try harder."

"Look, Q, I don't owe you shit. I don't have to do nothing for you."

He uncrossed his legs and was about to re-cross them.

"Could you not do that?" Jada said.

"Do what?"

"Cross your legs."

"Why?"

"It's so gay."

"Whatever." He crossed them anyway.

"I need you to get in touch with Starr."

"I tried."

"She has my baby, damn it!"

"I don't know anything about that."

"You think I'll tell her that you told me."

Jada eyebrows raised. "I didn't tell you shit."

"What is she doing, Jada? Why won't she answer the phone?"

"Why didn't you answer the phone when she called you?"

"So you have spoken to her?"

"Maybe."

"Is she thinking about aborting my baby?"

"I don't know nothing about that."

"So you're going to act dumb?"

"Q, look, I have no idea what you are talking about."

He stood and he marched to the door wearing those salmon-colored pants. She wanted to laugh at his metrosexual ass. He's Starr's man, not hers. There was no way she would deal with a man wearing pink pants and crossing his legs. She didn't think he was gay but damn, he had some bitch-like tendencies. She called Fresh as soon as Q left.

"Bae."

"You had to go running your goddamned mouth."

"What are you talking about?"

"Told Q that Starr was pregnant."

"She's going to tell him anyway, right?"

"Maybe. Maybe not."

"What is that supposed to mean?"

"Look, man, I told you not to say shit and you did the exact opposite of what I asked you to do."

"Look, having a baby is big news."

"Damn, Fresh, now if he goes back and tells Starr this shit, it's going to be like I'm telling her business."

"He's not going to say anything"

* * *

Eight p.m. and the moon hung low and the sky was full of blazing stars Brooke sat between DeMontre's legs on the hood of her car. His finger was in the pocket of her jeans. He cupped her ass with his free hand and he was biting on her neck. Her Dolce and Gabbana light blue perfume smelled just wonderful to him.

He said, "I wish we could freeze this moment in time."

"I was thinking the same thing."

Their chests pressed together. Their heartbeats in sync. "I don't know, shawty. I was thinking we both seventeen and pretty soon I know your folks is probably going to send you away to school and I won't get to see you no more."

"I can go to school in Atlanta."

His eyes lit up and he smiled. "You would do that?"

"I would, baby! That way I can still work for your auntie. She pays me damn good for a kid my age."

"How much does she pay you?"

"I'm not telling you."

"Afraid I'm going to ask you for it?"

"Just say I make more than a lot of adults."

"Damn! Auntie got it like that?"

"She's good at what she does. And she teaches me a lot too. At first I didn't like it, but I love it now."

"Interior decorating?"

"Interior design."

"Same thing." He laughed and then said, "Seriously, even if you went to school here, shawty, it will be just a matter of time before things fall apart with us."

She took a step back and said, "Stop being so negative."

"Not being negative. It's just the truth. I mean I'm a trap boy and that's all I'm going to ever be."

"You can be whatever you want to be in life."

He laughed and said, "You sound like Iyanla Vansant."

"You got jokes."

"I'm just kidding, shawty. I don't think I want to be anything else."

"Don't say that."

"It's true. I mean I can't rap. I'm too small to play ball. This is it."

"But you're smart, DeMontre. "

"So I've been told."

"Get your GED and enroll in college."

"Maybe one day."

Warmth radiated through her body as he gripped her ass again. He stepped back and said, "I know, you gotta go home."

She sighed and said, "Yeah, I have to get ready for school in the morning."

He had never felt like this about anyone in his young life. He could stare at her all night and still be infatuated. He had never expected her to like him. Girls like her just didn't talk to guys like him. He held her hands, wishing they could stay seventeen, but he knew that every second that went by he was getting older and older.

"Why are you smiling?" Brooke asked.

"You make me feel so alive."

"What are you thinking?"

"You look incredible, shawty."

She blushed. She was happy that he had noticed. She didn't usually wear makeup, but at the last moment, she had decided to add some lip gloss.

"Another kiss before you leave me?" He held her hand.

"What if I don't wanna?"

"But you do."

She smiled and said, "I do."

DeMontre planted his lips on hers. Suddenly, the sound of police sirens echoed throughout the hood. Seconds later, three police cars approached them. A K-9 unit and two unmarked cars. DeMontre prompted her to move away from him, dug into his pocket and removed a baggie full of crack rocks. He let go of them onto the streets and kicked the drugs under her car.

He was about to sprint down the street when a black police officer named Stevens with an adequate, well-groomed beard aimed his gun at DeMontre.

"Don't move." Stevens said.

Brooke was startled and she just stood there, not knowing what to do.

A Latina officer named Reyes approached Brooke. "What is your name, ma'am?"

"Brooke Latecomer."

"Can I see your ID?"

Brooke handed the woman her driver's license.

"A long way from the hood."

"Yeah."

"Rich girl, what you doing in the hood?"

"I'm not rich."

"But you don't need to be around here."

"She's my girl," DeMontre said.

Stevens cuffed DeMontre.

"Why are you arresting him? He hasn't done anything."

Sixteen officers bombarded the trap house. The officer ordered Brooke to get back in her car.

"I have to go home. I have to go to school in the morning."

Reyes and Stevens laughed at Brooke. "You see, it don't work like that around here. You are going to be here until we finish our investigation. You can call your parents and tell them that you're in the hood in front of a trap house that's getting searched if you want to."

Stevens shined his light near the tires of her car and spotted a bag of rocks. He held it up in the air. "You want to tell us whose this is?" he asked.

"What is that?" Brooke said.

Reyes laughed. "The fact that you don't know what this is, lets me know you're in the wrong neighborhood."

"If it ain't yours, it must be your boyfriend's." Stevens turned to DeMontre. "Is this yours?"

DeMontre didn't respond.

The cop said to Brooke, "You know how this works, don't you? If he don't own up to this, you're taking a nice little ride downtown. You wanna tell us what you know?"

Brooke wondered how she was going to explain this to her parents. If she got a criminal record, all her hopes and dreams would be over, and DeMontre's ass was over there not saying a damn word. She crossed her arms.

DeVante, Marco and four crackheads were paraded outside in plexicuffs. They were ordered to lay face down in the yard.

The officers searched the house thoroughly and didn't find a damn thing inside the house. But there was still the bag of crack that DeMontre refused to acknowledge.

Stevens ordered them to remove the plexicuffs from DeVante and the crackheads. Then he turned to Brooke. "You want to tell us about this bag of crack that was found near your car."

"I don't know anything."

He then turned back to the boyfriend and said, "Somebody knows something."

"I don't know shit."

Stevens ordered Reyes to cuff Brooke, and when he placed the cuffs on Brooke, she started crying.

"I don't know anything about this."

DeMontre said, "Hey, let her go. It's mine."

Reyes removed the cuffs from Brooke's wrists and said, "Get the hell away from here and don't ever come back to this neighborhood."

Chapter 23

"WHY HAVE YOU BEEN AVOIDING MY CALLS?" Q SAID. HE
had finally caught up to Starr. She had been trying to enter
her shop through the back of the showroom.

Starr turned and faced him. She wasn't expecting to see
him, but she knew that she couldn't go on avoiding him.
She needed to have a conversation with him. She sat her
briefcase down. She looked disappointed.

"You've been crying?" Q asked.

"You can tell?"

He tried to embrace her and she said, "Get away."

"Look, I'm sorry about what happened."

"What are you talking about?"

"I'm sorry I was acting like an ass."

She smirked. And as much as she hated to admit it, she
had wanted to hear him apologize.

"You hurt my feelings."

"I admit I was wrong."

"You made me feel so low, Quentin."

"I'm sorry. I was just thinking of myself. When you told me
you slept with the basketball player, I was devastated."

"I'm too honest."

"I like that."

"Men can't take honesty."

He laughed and said, "We really can't. There is a lot of shit we say we want to know, but we really don't want to hear it."

"Look, I slept with him because you said you had slept with that Chanel girl."

"And you think that was going to solve anything?"

"Look, I was lonely and vulnerable and he was attractive."

"You are attracted to him?"

"I want you."

"But you said he was attractive."

"He is but I don't want him. I want you."

He embraced her. This time she didn't resist. "I want you." He kissed her forehead. "I missed you."

"If you missed me, then why didn't you answer the phone when I called you?"

"You hurt my feelings."

"You're such a sensitive man."

"When it comes to you, I am."

She blushed then picked up her briefcase and said, "I have to open up."

"So why were you sad?"

"I don't want to talk about it."

"I want to know."

She sighed and said, "I'm pregnant."

"What?"

A huge grin covered his face though he already knew, but he had to pretend he didn't know because if he told her that Fresh told him, then she would know it came from Jada. And though Jada had basically called him gay, he wasn't going to put her in a bad position.

"Why ain't you happy?"

"I don't know what I'm going to do."

"What do you mean?"

"Q, me and you are in a bad space. Although I want a baby, I don't know if the situation is right."

"The situation is never right for a kid. You make it right."

"When was the last time you seen your kids in Houston?"

"Oh, that was a low blow."

"Wasn't meant to be low. I'm just saying kids need two parents."

"You're right."

"What do you want me to do?"

He avoided her eyes. "It really don't matter what I say about it. It's all about what the woman says. She has the final decision."

"Don't feel like that, bae."

"It's true."

"I'm going to pray about it."

He gave her a peck on the forehead and said, "You do that."

Chapter 24

WITH THE PRODUCT THAT DANIELS HAD GIVEN BLACK, he'd profited himself over fifty thousand dollars. And it took him only a day to make it. Big Ced knew some people in South Carolina. Once the South Carolina boys found out that it was pure, they wanted to take all he had.

Bird had been pressing him about the money and Black was going to pay him, but he felt like Bird was trying to make him into a little bitch. Plus, Black just didn't like Bird's demeanor. While he did want to get Avant's ass back, he didn't feel like he owed Bird shit. Bird called him three times back to back and Black finally answered him.

"Hello?"

"I thought we had a deal?"

"Look, bruh, we can meet tomorrow and make the exchange. Just let me know where you want to meet at."

"My homie got a motorcycle club in Lithonia. You cool with that?"

"I'm cool with it."

"What time is good for you?"

"Nine thirty."

"Make sure you have all the money."

"I'll have it."

"Cool."

Black hung up the phone. He had a meeting with Daniels and he drove to the meeting spot. This time Daniels drove a black Dodge Ram. He greeted Black who was still uneasy. Although he somewhat trusted this man, he was still the police. Black was still suspecting that he was being tricked and that the police was going to take him to jail sooner or later.

"Where's the bread?" Daniels asked.

Black passed him the bag of money.

"Do I need to count it?"

"It's all there. Why the SUV?"

"I got marijuana this time."

"What?"

"Look, I have to get you what I can get you. I busted some Arizona dudes with two thousand pounds of weed."

"Damn. I ain't no weed dealer."

"You can't sell it?"

"I can. I'll just have to get the word out."

"Look, just do what you can."

"So, the weed is on the back of the truck inside the cab?"

"Yup."

"Nobody is going to jump out and arrest me, are they?"

Daniels laughed and said, "Hell no, Black. We on the same team."

Daniels popped open the back and grabbed a duffle bag. He ordered Black to get the other two and they tossed them into the back of Black's car.

"I can tell you right now, there is no way I can put two thousand pounds in this car."

Daniels said, "I only bought about two hundred. Just to see how it goes and if you want more, I'll get it for you."

"Okay, cool."

He and Black loaded the weed into the trunk of Black's car. They shook hands and Black sped off.

• • •

Miss America jerked Craig's dick in an attempt to make it erect again. She'd given him some incredible oral and he'd exploded in her mouth. After fifteen minutes of caressing his tiny pink penis, she gave up. They lay in the bed and he had one hand on her ass while stroking her green weave with the other. It was nighttime and he was about to doze off. Then he rolled over to the coke and straw on the stand and he snorted some of it down.

"You know, I really don't like your green hair," Craig said.

She rolled over and faced him. There was a speck of powder on his nose like there always seemed to be.

"You know, I really don't give a damn what you like until you start paying for my hair. I will get what I want. TeTe told me not to see your ass again, anyway."

"So why did you see me again?"

"Look, I needed the money; otherwise, I wouldn't be here." She looked at the clock, waiting for Fy-head and J-Will to burst into the room and snatch Craig's ass up. Fy-head was fifteen minutes behind and she was starting to get nervous.

"You don't like me at all?"

"Kinda."

"You do."

She smiled. "I do."

"But not enough to tell me where your friend is hiding?"

"I don't know where she is hiding. I already told you this." She turned her back, her ass faced him now.

He attempted to stroke her hair and she said, "Don't touch me. You don't like my hair, remember?"

"I just don't like the color."

"So you don't like green hair?"

"I don't."

"And I don't like red noses and white lines."

He wanted to ask about the whereabouts of Fy-Head but he didn't. Instead he said, "Why make your hair green?"

"Could you find something else to talk about?"

"I just asked you a question?"

"I colored it green because I would like to think of myself as a mermaid."

"A mermaid? Why a mermaid?"

"I think I was born with the wrong part below."

"Oh wow. How creative."

"It's not creative. It's a fact that lots of FTM transgendered identify as mermaids."

He snorted another line of coke from the dresser using the straw.

"Can you pay me? I need to go." She stood and he watched her as she got dressed. She slid into a pair of jeans and some stilettos and for the first time, he could tell she was born a man. Her feet were huge. After she put her shoes on, she primped her hair in the mirror.

She turned and saw him still staring at her. "Will you quit looking at me?"

"What's wrong?"

"You just weird me out."

"I weird you out? You just said that you kinda liked me."

"I lied." She held her hand out and said, "Can I have my money and you need to reimburse me for the room."

Craig plopped down on his knees and retrieved his pants from underneath the bed. He fished out eighteen one hundred dollar bills and passed them to Miss America who recounted the money before making a beeline to the door. When she turned the doorknob, a bearded white man wearing a biker jacket barged through the door.

When he closed the door, she saw that his jacket had a skull with a pirate hat and patch across the skeleton. The name Demonic Bastards was etched above the artwork.

Miss America was trembling so bad, she almost forgot that there was a mini .45 in her purse. She removed it from her purse and fired a shot that ripped through the biker's bicep.

Craig sprang from the bed trying to contain her but she was too strong. She was a man. Blood leaked from the biker's biceps but he managed to remove his silver .45 and fire two shots. Both shots ripped right through Miss America's chest. Her heart stopped beating on impact and she crashed face first to the floor.

Craig said, "Oh shit, you think somebody heard that?"

"I'm sure somebody heard her gun. Why didn't you tell me the bitch had a gun?"

"I didn't know."
"We gotta get the fuck out of here."
Craig struggled with his pants and shoes.
"What about this body?" the biker said.
"We can't carry the goddamned body out in the lobby. What about a suitcase?"
"Look, hotel security is coming, I'm sure."
"We're fucked."

•   •   •

It was shortly after eight when TeTe entered Starbuck's to meet with John, the pervert, again. He was dumping a pack of Splenda into a latte when TeTe approached the table.
John said, "That girl's tits were too big."
TeTe sat down and said, "John, look, none of my girls wear training bras. What the fuck? Nobody has time to find you adolescents and you know I don't play that shit anyways."
He laughed and said, "You know I don't want no adolescent."
"Look, John, that was the youngest looking girl I got. Either you take it or you leave it."
"I took it."
"Okay."
"I'm just saying that's not what I like."
"Can we talk about what we came here for?"
"Yes, of course." He was stirring his coffee.
"Did you clean up the mess?"
"I cleaned up the mess and destroyed the cell phone."
"Nobody saw you, right?"
"Nobody and there no signs of a murder. No DNA fibers. Nothing."
"You're the best, John."
His face became serious and when she noticed it she said, "What's wrong?"
"I couldn't find Rakeem and Jabril."
"Why not?"
"I don't know. Maybe those names aren't their birth names. I'm going to find them though. I just gotta do more digging."

"You can't pull up an address on them?"

"Nothing."

"What are you thinking?"

"I think they may have been born with regular names like Kevin or Mark and maybe their father decided to become Muslim and changed his kid's names. It happens all the time. I'll find them. Just give me about a week."

"I don't have a week. These motherfuckers want to kill me and I need to find them and take them out before they take me out."

"I understand and I'll do my best."

"Find them and I'll find you that training bra bitch that you want."

He was laughing his ass off. "It's not that simple."

She looked at him with cold icy eyes and said, "Find them."

"Give me a week."

Chapter 25

The room was freezing and Starr rubbed her arms with both hands trying to generate some body heat. Starr sat on the doctor's table wearing a blue hospital gown, wondering what her future would hold. Would she be with Q? Did she really want to have a baby? Or did she want to abort the baby? She had waited so long to become pregnant, only to be relegated to being a baby mama. The door opened and Dr. Melton entered the room. Dr. Tamara Melton had been Starr's gynecologist for the last six years. She was a petite, copper-colored woman with long natural hair. She wore designer glasses and had a pleasant demeanor. Tamara smiled brilliantly when she entered the room. She shuffled the papers that she was carrying and then looked at Starr.

"You're definitely pregnant," Dr. Melton said.

"Well, I kind of figured that."

"Well, in some cases, the home pregnancy test is wrong. Not often, but sometimes."

Tamara smiled so hard you could see her entire mouth. "I'm so happy for you."

"Me too," Starr said.

"You don't seem like it."

"I guess it hasn't sunk in yet."

"Well, you got about seven months to get ready."

"Seven months? How far along am I?" Starr's face was concerned. She hopped off the table and grabbed her clothes that were on the chair.

"Six weeks."

"What?"

"Yeah, six weeks."

"How accurate is your test?"

"My test is a hundred percent accurate."

"No, I'm taking about the date."

"Well, there is no way I can give you an exact date, but it's pretty close."

Starr did the math in her head. Although she'd had sex with Q twice in the last couple of weeks, there was no way that this baby was his. And that could mean only one thing—the baby was Terrell's. How could she explain this to Q? Now she would have to let him know that she was pregnant by Terrell. Starr dropped her head.

•   •   •

Jada stared at Tank's muscled back. He was sleeping so peaceful and she didn't want to wake him, but she knew that he had to go home to his girlfriend. He had been wanting to spend more time with her. He was starting to get attached. She liked Tank and she could see herself with him, but she really liked Fresh. But Fresh just liked to play around, and she knew that there was no future there, especially since he had shown that he can, and will, gossip like a bitch. Her phone rang. It was TeTe, but she didn't answer.

Tank turned over on his back and began snoring. She was thinking how nice it would be if he could spend the night. She missed having a man to hold her all night. A man that actually wanted her.

TeTe called again.

This time she picked up. "Hello?"

"I'm on my way over."

"Whoa, Whoa, Whoa. What's going on?"

Jada heard someone crying in the background.

"I would rather talk to you in person."

The first thing Jada thought was that maybe something happened to Black.

"Ok, come over. You're going to have to be quiet. I have company."

Jada decided that she could let Tank's ass oversleep. Let his bitch wonder where he's at.

Jada slipped on a pair of booty shorts and a wife beater. Ten minutes later, TeTe arrived with Fy-Head who was sobbing. They sat down in the living room and Jada offered them drinks. They declined.

"What is going on?" Jada asked.

TeTe said, "Jada, that white man that you used to fuck? Craig?"

Jada got up from her seat and made sure that the door was closed. The last thing she needed was Tank to hear what they were discussing. He didn't need to know that she used to fuck Craig or nobody else for that matter.

Jada took her position back on the sofa. "What about him?"

"Look, we have big problems, Jada."

"What are you talking about? We?"

"Look, I think Craig murdered Miss America."

Fy-head said, "I know he murdered her."

Jada looked confused. "He murdered her? What do you mean he murdered her?"

Fy-head said, "Look, a few weeks ago, I met with him and her and he asked us if we knew somebody who could do a job for him."

"What kind of job?"

"He wanted his wife murdered."

Jada kept listening and she could definitely believe that he wanted his wife murdered. She remembered conversations that she had had with him about his wife trying to take everything that he had. He believed that she was the reason that he had fell on hard times.

Fy-Head continued. "And so I said I had someone."

"He paid you?"

"Yes."

"Okay, he came here a few weeks ago. I don't know how in the hell he found me, but he came here a few weeks ago, wanting me to get in touch with you."

"I knew he was looking for me."

"So I guess you took the money and didn't do the job?"

"Yeah." Fy-Head was crying and Jada said, "You're going to have to hold it down. I have company."

"I'm sorry, Jada. I'm sorry we came to your house."

"What can I do to help?"

"Do you know where we can find him?"

"I haven't dealt with that man in a long time." Jada huffed and said, "Look, he hired you to do a job so I know you know where his wife lives. Why don't you ask there? And I know the hotel has surveillance. It's just a matter of time before the police catch him."

TeTe stood and paced. "I don't want them to catch him. If they catch him, they investigate and find out that she is an escort. Then the cops start digging all in my business and shit and then they're going to want to shut me down and try to charge me. I don't need the cops on my ass. You understand me?"

"Look, I don't know where he is. I don't talk to the man. I don't understand why you're here."

TeTe said, "Look, Jada, I thought you could be still fucking the man. I don't know."

Jada said, "Get the fuck out of my house."

"I'm sorry, Jada."

"Please leave, TeTe."

TeTe made eye contact with Jada again and said, "I'm really sorry for what I said."

"It's okay," Jada said.

"We good?"

"We good."

Chapter 26

THE SMELL OF PREMIUM MARIJUANA WAFTED THROUGH the car. What a Time To Be Alive by Future & Drake was blaring through the speakers. Black approached the traffic light on Old National and passed the cigar to Big Ced.

Big Ced inhaled and said, "Yo, I forgot to tell you. Those little dudes that we pressed the other day? Their house got raided."

"What?"

"Yeah, one of them went to jail."

Black inhaled the blunt and said, "I don't know them. Those were Q's problem."

Black and Ced loaded the clips of their guns.

Big Ced said, "I really don't get it, man. So you're going to pay these dudes fifty stacks to turn this dude over to you. Why, when you could have gotten him yourself?"

"Not exactly. A partna of mine tried to stick them up and they killed him but it cost them fifty thousand cuz the police found their stash after the shots were fired."

"So they want you to pay them for that?"

"Yeah."

"Sounds like extortion. Look, bruh. I can get a team of

goons and we can handle this."

Bird had called Black and told him where they would meet. He put Avant on the phone. But Black didn't want to meet Bird and the boy alone. He didn't trust him. They would meet at a trailer park in Fayette, Georgia. Black and Big Ced would go and Black had a crew waiting about a mile up the road from the scene. Black and Big Ced rolled up to the mobile home at the end of a dirt road. There were two cars, a cream-colored, two-seater Bentley and a red Maserati parked in front of the trailer.

Bird and another man were standing outside and Avant was standing between both of them with a rope around his neck and his hands tied behind his back.

When Black rolled up, they cocked their guns and exited the vehicle.

Bird walked over and shook Black's hand and he sized up Big Ced without speaking. Then he said, "You got the bread?"

Black moseyed his way back to the vehicle and got the money. He gave Bird the briefcase and said, "Here is the money."

Two men jumped out of the back of the Bentley.

Black said, "What the fuck is this?"

Black reached for his weapon and the smaller of the two men said, "Drop the gun or I kill you."

Black dropped his gun but Big Ced held on to his.

Black said, "Drop the gun, man."

"Fuck that. They're going to kill us anyway."

Bird thumbed through the money. When he closed the briefcase, Bird glanced at one of his men. "Kill the motherfucker."

The big guy fired a shot into Avant's skull.

Black said, "What the fuck was that all about?"

"Look, I wanted what I lost."

"So why couldn't we get Avant?"

"Because we wanted him. He set us up to get robbed, so he had to pay."

Bird said, "I'm going to tell you one time, homie. Lower the gun or you don't leave here alive."

"I got my money and we got Avant. So I have no beef with you."

"You're lying, bruh."

Four more Crips, dressed in khakis and blue bandanas came storming out of the trailer and they all had guns.

Bird said, "So you see? The only chance you got to get out of here alive is dropping your gun."

Black walked up to Big Ced and said, "Drop your gun."

He looked around and finally he dropped the gun and the little dude fired a shot in his kneecap.

Black said, "You said you wouldn't shoot!"

Bird said, "We didn't kill him, did we? Now get the fuck away from here before we bury y'all bitches."

Black picked up Big Ced who was bleeding like slaughtered livestock and tossed him in the back of the car before speeding off. Ced was moaning in the back of the car and he was losing a lot of blood. Black still had time to get him to the hospital. He picked up his phone and dialed his help.

"They at a trailer at the end of the road. You'll see two cars, a Bentley and a red Maserati."

*   *   *

Tank rolled over and glanced at Jada's clock. It read seven forty-five. Then he stared at the ceiling before realizing that he was not at home. He was not in his bed. The ceiling he stared at was not his.

He sprang from the bed and began searching frantically for his pants. Where was his shoe? Where was he? Then he realized he was at Jada's home and Jada's naked body lay frozen in the bed. Her hair was wrapped and her back looked so beautiful and sensual. That incredible ass made him want to crawl back into the bed for morning sex. His morning erection was certainly ready for action.

He spotted his phone on the nightstand. He picked it up. It was off. He tried to power it on but it would not start. The battery was completely drained and he was fucked because he was sure that his kids' mother had tried to reach him. He grabbed Jada's shoulder and she turned over to see him.

With one eye open, she said, "What's wrong?"

"I overslept."

She sat up on the bed. "I'm sorry."

"It's okay." He was struggling to put his pants on. Then his Chuck Taylors. His watch and bracelet was on the nightstand by the phone.

Jada made a sad face. "You're in trouble?"

"No. I mean, yeah."

She laughed. "Are you afraid?"

"No."

"What are you going to tell her?"

He laughed and said, "I had some of the best pussy in Atlanta."

"Don't tell her that. I don't want to have to whoop nobody's ass."

"I need to gargle some mouthwash. You got any?"

"There is an extra toothbrush in the medicine cabinet and mouthwash under the sink."

"Perfect."

"I'll fix you something to eat."

"I don't have time."

"Look, you're already fucked. Might as well eat."

"I'll get something at Chick-fil-A."

"Processed food?"

"That's all I have time for."

"Okay."

Tank brushed his teeth and gargled down some mouthwash. "I thought I told you to wake me up?"

She smiled.

"So you let me oversleep?"

"Fuck your girlfriend."

"What, Jada? Are you serious?"

"I like competition."

"Huh?"

"Well I seen her and she really ain't no competition."

"Ah, Jada, that's fucked up." He made a beeline to the living room and she trailed him. She was still butt naked and before he reached the door, he turned and kissed her. His hands cupped her ass and he whispered, "Damn, I don't want to go now."

"Make me into a believer."

"I'll be back."

She smiled. "Sure."

He left and she locked the door and went to the bathroom to pee.

The doorbell rang. Jada got up and walked to the door. Tank must have left something.

"Who is it?"

"It's the police. We're looking for Jada Simone."

Why were they here? Had Tank's girlfriend sent them here? She couldn't have sent them to her house. She didn't know where Jada lived.

Jada said, "Let me slip on some clothes."

Jada ran to the bedroom and put on a pair of jeans and a T-shirt. Seconds later, she opened the door.

"How can I help you?"

"Can we come in?"

"Please do."

"You know Craig Matthews?"

"I do."

"When was the last time you saw him?"

"Why?"

"Dr. Matthews's wife was murdered last night."

"Wait a goddamned minute. I don't know nothing about that."

"We know, but we want a few minutes of your time."

To be continued

GET A FREE eBOOK!

Enjoyed this book?
If you enjoyed this book please write a review and email it to me at kevinelliott3@gmail.com, and get a FREE ebook.

K. Elliott Book Order Form
PO Box 12714
Charlotte NC 28220

Book Name	Quantity	Price	Shipping/Handling	Total
Dear Summer		X $14.95	+ $3.00 per book	
Dilemma		X $14.95	+ $3.00 per book	
Entangled		X $13.95	+ $3.00 per book	
Godsend Series 1–5		X $14.95	+ $3.00 per book	
Godsend Series 6–10		X $14.95	+ $3.00 per book	
Kingpin Wifeys Vol. 1		X $14.95	+ $3.00 per book	
Kingpin Wifeys Vol. 2		X $14.95	+ $3.00 per book	
Kingpin Wifeys Vol. 3		X $14.95	+ $3.00 per book	
Kingpin Wifeys Vol. 4		X $14.95	+ $3.00 per book	
Kingpin Wifeys Vol. 5		X $14.95	+ $3.00 per book	
Kingpin Wifeys Vol. 6		X $14.95	+ $3.00 per book	
Street Fame		X $14.95	+ $3.00 per book	
Treasure Hunter		X $15.00	+ $3.00 per book	
			TOTAL	

Mailing Address

Name:

Mailing Address:

City	State	Zip

Method Of Payment
[   ] Check [   ] Money Order

Thank you for your support

About the Author

K. Elliott, aka The Well Fed Black Writer, penned his first novel, Entangled, in 2003. Although he was offered multiple signing deals, Elliott decided to found his own publishing company, Urban Lifestyle Press.

Bookstore by bookstore, street vendor by street vendor, Elliott took to the road selling his story. He did not go unnoticed, selling 50,000 units in his first year and earning a spot on the Essence Magazine Bestsellers list.

Since Entangled, Elliott has published five titles of his own and two more on behalf of authors signed to Urban Lifestyle Press. For one book, The Ski Mask Way, Elliott was selected to co-author with hip-hop superstar 50 Cent. Along the way, he has continued to look for innovative ways to push his books to his fans while keeping down his overhead.

Elliott is passionate about sharing what he has learned with aspiring authors, and has conducted learning webinars filled with information on what works best for him. He is the author of numerous best-sellers including Dilemma, Street Fame, Treasure Hunter, Dear Summer, Entangled, The Godsend Series and the hugely intriguing Kingpin Wifeys Series.